The Old Left

The Old Left

Stories by
Daniel Menaker

Alfred A. Knopf   New York   1987

THIS IS A BORZOI BOOK
PUBLISHED BY ALFRED A. KNOPF, INC.

Copyright © 1982, 1984, 1987 by Daniel Menaker

All rights reserved under International and Pan-American Copyright Conventions. Published in the United States by Alfred A. Knopf, Inc., New York, and simultaneously in Canada by Random House of Canada Limited, Toronto. Distributed by Random House, Inc., New York.

Most of the stories in this book were originally published in *The New Yorker*. "The Old Left" and "Brothers" were originally published in *Grand Street*.

Library of Congress Cataloging-in-Publication Data

Menaker, Daniel.
The old left.

Most stories appeared originally
in the New Yorker.
I. Title.
PS3563.E4604   1987   813'.54   86-46020
ISBN 0-394-54678-4

Manufactured in the United States of America
FIRST EDITION

For William Maxwell

Whatever quality these stories may have, I can say with certainty they would have had much less without the clear, sane, and encouraging criticism they received from my wife, Katherine Bouton. The love and humanity she has brought to my work she has also brought to me and to our lives together, and I am grateful to her beyond measure.

I deeply appreciate the support and acumen of Frances Kiernan, my editor at *The New Yorker;* Ben Sonnenberg, the editor of *Grand Street,* and my friend; and Alice Quinn, of Alfred A. Knopf. And I thank my son, William, for helping me to relocate certain pieces of my heart which I had begun to fear might be permanently misplaced. And Leon Chattah, for so rigorously asking me to try to be honest.

Contents

The Old Left

Brothers

I

DAVID LEONARD WAS TWENTY-SIX. He taught English at a good private boys' school in Manhattan. His brother, Nicholas, was twenty-nine and worked as an associate in a Wall Street law firm.

Nick was fairer than Dave, and taller and thicker. Dave had a dark complexion and curly dark hair. Nick could fix small things, Dave's handwriting was impatient-looking and crude. Nick told stories, Dave joked. Nick was married, organized, cautious; Dave could listen to the same rock-and-roll song or even just the ending to the same song fifteen times.

On Thanksgiving Day Nick and Dave were playing touch football on the lawn in front of their parents' house, in Palisades, New York. The drab-green lawn stretched from the front of the house to the very edge of the Hudson River, which on this day was chopped into sharp, angry-looking waves by a chilly north wind. The brothers were playing against two rich cousins from Boston, John and Daniel Randolph. Nick's wife, Nancy, looked on as the four young men had their fun. Louise Carter, Dave's girlfriend, stood near the river, her back to the house, her shoulders drawn in against the wind, and gazed over the water. Louise, who was from South Carolina, had been two years behind Dave in college, and after she graduated she came to New York to try to be an actress. They were always talking about getting married.

Nick had a bad right knee, so Dave had to play backfield on defense and receiver on offense. He was getting worn out, and finally he said to Nick, "Why don't you play pass defense for once. Your precious knee will hold up." Nick said, O.K., he would. On the next play, John went out for a pass. He and Nick got themselves into a cartoonlike tangle of arms and legs when they went up for the ball. Both young men were tall and solid, and when they hit the ground, Dave felt a vibration through his feet, as if from an earthquake two hundred miles away. Nick came down with his right leg bent, and he cried out in pain. Nancy ran to where he lay on the ground, grimacing and shaking his head as if he could refuse the injury, and as she rolled up the leg of his jeans, she gave Dave a filthy glare.

"Look at that," she said. "Maybe it's not so bad."

"It's bad enough," Nick said as Nancy poked at his knee. "Jesus, Nance, what are you doing?"

Dave, who had been pacing around fifteen yards away, now walked over to Nick. "Defensive interference," he said.

"That's really funny," Nancy said.

"Help me up, Davey," Nick said. "I can't walk on this thing."

Dave took Nick's hand and hauled him upright. Nick draped his arm over Dave's shoulder. After a few steps, Nick said, "Wait a minute. My leg is freezing." He bent over and rolled down his jeans. Dave looked over the lawn to where Louise was standing, oblivious of what had happened. With her back still to the house, she turned three cartwheels, her long hair streaming out like a black pennant.

. . .

Nick was to be operated on in a Brooklyn hospital on the tenth of December by an orthopedic surgeon who was a friend of the family's. Dave had misgivings about the doctor and the hospital but felt that he had already caused enough trouble and kept his mouth shut. The night before the operation, Dave, who had come down with a mild strep throat, called Nick in the hospital. "I'm really sorry about all this," he said, in a raspy voice.

"Oh, you sensitive asshole," Nick said. "Forget about it."

"I shouldn't have made you play backfield."

"The day you make me do anything," Nick said.

"When's the operation?" Dave asked.

"Seven tomorrow morning. I'm sort of scared."

"Don't be ridiculous," Dave said. "It wasn't bad the first time you had it."

"It hurt like a bitch for a whole week afterward. You couldn't have stood it, Mister Delicate. You would have been a real case. The pain, the pain."

"*¡Qué lástima!*" Dave said. "Did I tell you I was tutoring one of the kids at school in Spanish? P.S., he's Puerto Rican. He speaks street Spanish, and—"

"Wait, here's Nancy. Listen, I'll talk to you tomorrow or the next day. In extreme agony."

"Come on," Dave said. "You'll be O.K."

When Nick Leonard had married Nancy, two years earlier, Dave felt as if some strange kind of operation had hollowed out part of his body. It was ridiculous, he knew, but he imagined that he could actually locate the site of the loss; it was on his left side, from the inner part of his upper arm, up and under his armpit, and then down along his rib cage—a shape like the winning two-thirds of a used wishbone. Dave was Nick's best man at the wedding, which took place at Nancy's parents' big house in Mount

Kisco, and only two things went wrong: he forgot to include a shirt with Nick's traveling clothes, so that one of the guests of Nick's size had to lend him his; and during the ceremony Dave felt an ache in his ribs, as if the minister were a juju man working on the marrow of his bones.

The wedding did nothing but further attenuate the bond between the two brothers, which had already grown thin and tense. From the time that Dave had begun teaching and Nick had started at the law firm and met Nancy, the roughhousing, the sharp sarcasm, the ritual disputes about who was the smarter, the more athletic, the better-looking all withered away. When Dave tried to revive them, he almost always ended up feeling stupid and embarrassed, as if he had told a joke that nobody laughed at.

Nick had been born when their mother, Emily, was thirty-seven; Dave, when she was forty. She went back to her job as chief copy editor for an art magazine soon after, leaving them largely in the care of a loving and garrulous black woman. Their father, Joseph, struggled at being an institutional-insurance salesman, traveling throughout South America on business when they were young.

The boys were raised to call their parents Emily and Joe and not to call on God at all. They lived in Greenwich Village and went to a progressive school. Joe was the youngest son of two radical Russian-Jewish immigrants. Emily, who came from a wealthy Philadelphia Quaker family, listened patiently to Joe's righteous complaints, indulging him just as she indulged her boys.

Dave grew into adolescence sensing that things in his family were not as they ought to be, and not knowing that they never were in any family. The constant in his life was his brother.

On the day of Nick's operation, Dave's strep throat got worse, and by the time he met the ten seniors in his advanced English class, after lunch, he sounded like a movie villain.

"The last time, we started to talk about 'Ode on a Grecian

Urn,'" he croaked, "and I asked each of you to write in a single sentence what you thought Keats was trying to say in it—what its theme was—and to be ready to back it up with evidence from—Tim, put your hand down or you'll lose the circulation in it. We're going to do this in alphabetical order."

"I guess I've got to be prepared to go through the rest of my life like this," Ken Aaron said. "'The Ode on a Grecian Urn' is about a beautiful urn, or large vase, with various paintings on it that show how art is better than real life," Ken said.

"Yes, maybe," Dave said, "but what is 'Ode on a Grecian Urn' about?"

"I just told you, sir," Ken said.

"No, you told us what '*The* Ode on a Grecian Urn' was about. Now, Danny Heisler." Dave got up and started pacing.

"'Ode on a Grecian Urn' is about time—how you can't live or be happy in it or outside of it."

Dave stopped and squinted at Danny, his favorite. "Didn't I teach your brother Nick—I mean, Mike—this poem two years ago?"

"He's not even home from vacation yet, sir. This is my own idea. You have a suspicious nature, sir."

"Sir, that was my idea, too," Tim Shaffer said.

"That I have a suspicious nature?"

Another teacher came into the room. There was a call for Dave on the public phone on the first floor.

It was his mother calling from the hospital. "Nicky has a blood infection," she said. "He was operated on at seven-thirty this morning, and now he has a temperature of a hundred and five."

Dave, suddenly dizzy and cold, said, "O.K., I'll be there as soon as I can."

He hung up and called Louise, and told her what had happened. She said she would go to the hospital, too.

· · ·

The hospital was way out in Brooklyn, in a neighborhood where the apartment houses were only five or six stories high, on broad gray avenues with too few cars and divided by mean, low concrete islands; the lampposts stuck out like a parade of cranes' legs—the only things that didn't look stepped-on.

As Dave walked down the hospital's long corridors, he came upon knots of two, three, four people—doctors and nurses and perhaps relatives—standing together and speaking quietly, nodding and inclining toward one another, heavy with plans. He saw his mother and father and the surgeon near the end of a long hall, outside Nick's room. Though she was shorter than the two men, Emily seemed to dominate them; there was some greater element of refinement in her bearing, in her mottled, craggy good looks. Joe stood next to her like a handsome escort. His hair was white with streaks of black, his nose was large and distinguished, but his eyes were reservoirs of deference. Joe draped his arm around Dave's shoulder. Emily tilted her head so Dave could kiss her on the cheek. The surgeon clasped Dave's hand with both of his.

"He was delirious for a while," Emily said. "They moved his roommate out because Nicky was—ranting. They've used an ice blanket to bring his temperature down. Do you want to see him?"

"Well, I'm still trying to get over this strep throat," Dave said.

"Then it might not be a good idea for you to see him," the surgeon said. "As I was telling your mother and father, some staph bug must have jumped in there during the operation, and now your brother has this septicemia."

"How long is it going to go on?" Dave said.

The surgeon explained Nick's condition. He looked relieved when a sound came out of his white coat. "My beeper," he said.

His place was taken, almost magically, by Louise and Nancy, the one girl lovely, with white skin and straight dark hair, looking the part of the actress she was trying to become, the other more conventionally pretty, wearing in the lapel of her tweedy jacket a pin of the logo of the large charity she worked for. They both had terrified smiles on their faces. "We came on the same subway," they said in unison, and everyone laughed loudly.

"Are we allowed to see him?" Nancy said.

Joe and Emily and Dave all said yes. More laughter, then silence, like the kind at a cocktail party following a *faux pas*.

"He's asleep, but it's all right to see him," Emily said.

Everyone moved toward Nick's room. Dave made Nancy stay out in the hall for a minute. "Are you angry at me?" he said.

"Oh, for heaven's sake, why should I be angry at you?" she said.

"Well, you were staring daggers at me after Nicky got hurt, and it was sort of my fault."

"I didn't know you performed the surgery," she said. Then she began to cry. Very tentatively, Dave put his arms around her. "Don't be ridiculous," she said through her tears. "It's not your fault at all."

Dave felt embarrassed holding his brother's wife. Her breasts against him, his hands on her narrow back.

At six, in the hideous, green-painted lounge near Nick's room, someone suggested that they should find the hospital's cafeteria and go there in two shifts. Dave said wouldn't it be better if he went out to a coffee shop and brought back some food. Louise offered to go with him.

It was cold on the street, and the strong wind drove a sandy, stinging snow down the avenue. Louise said, "Do you remember three summers ago when Nicky was living at home and studying for his bar exam? We were up in Palisades for the weekend and he wanted to go to the beach, but you didn't want to, so I went with him."

"And got a crush on him," Dave said.

"Now how did you know that?"

"Everyone I ever went out with who met Nicky got a crush on him. And vice versa, a little. We both have something that the other lacks, I guess."

"I think he got a little crush on me, too," Louise said.

"Why wouldn't he, two hours in the car and two hours on the beach with you in a bikini?" Dave said.

They passed under a streetlight and stopped at the curb. "You do realize that we're talking about him as if he were going to die," Dave said.

They found a dreary cafeteria-diner. The man behind the counter said, "Sorry, buddy, I'd like to help you but I don't have take-out." Dave said that his brother was in the hospital down the street, and wasn't there some way of taking something back to his parents? The man said, "Why didn't you say so in the first place? You don't sound so good yourself." He wrapped up some hamburgers and small salads. After they paid for the food, the counterman said, "Your brother is a young man?"

"Twenty-nine," Dave said.

"Then it isn't his heart?"

"No," Dave said. "He got a blood infection after a knee operation. It's called septicemia."

"But he's young, it isn't his heart, he'll be fine," the man said. "Up and around in no time."

"You really think so?" Dave said.

"No question about it."

At eleven that night, Dave and Joe went to the nurses' desk to hire a private nurse for Nick for the midnight shift. "Find a pretty one, like you," Joe said to the floor supervisor, a slender West Indian black woman.

"Mister, that boy could have his pick," she said. "He's got your looks."

As Dave and his father walked away from the nurses' station, Joe said, "I shouldn't have let Nicky come here."

"But it wasn't up to you, was it?" Dave said. "Listen, this is an accident," he went on, sawing the air with his hand in his best classroom manner. "Everyone can find a way to feel responsible if he tries hard enough, but it's no one's fault." He didn't believe a word of it.

"You sound very authoritative," Joe said. "Just like your mother."

They all tried to get some sleep in the lounge. After an hour or so of shifting around in one of the horrible chairs, Dave got up quietly and wandered the hospital's halls. Coming back to the lounge from a new direction, he found two service elevators hidden away in a sort of blind-alley corridor. Outside the elevators was a gurney bed covered with a clean sheet. He took off his sport coat, climbed up onto the bed, and lying on his back, drifted off into a restless sleep.

At dawn, Dave woke and went back to the lounge. Everyone else was still asleep, Emily and Joe on the couches, Louise and Nancy on the floor with chair cushions as makeshift pallets. As Dave was looking at them all, groggily, a resident came up to him.

"My brother?" Dave said.

"He's awake," the resident said. "He's not doing too well but you can see him."

"Well, I've got this strep throat," Dave said.

The doctor, a tall, sallow young man whose arms and legs seemed slightly out of his control, beckoned Dave out into the hall. "This situation will probably continue for a while," he said. "I just wanted to inform you that there's a residence for nurses and doctors across the street. One of the suites there may be available."

"It would be much better," Dave said, glancing back at the lounge.

The resident nodded his head once, sharply. He pivoted on

one heel, but as he walked away his arms and legs resumed living their own somewhat wayward lives. Then he came back and asked Dave if he wanted to go down to the Emergency Room with him for a shot of penicillin for his throat, and Dave said yes.

They would all need clean clothes and toothbrushes, and Louise had to go to her apartment in the Village to get ready for a TV-commercial audition. Dave volunteered to take Joe's car and drop Louise off, collect stuff from the house in Palisades, and then stop at his West Side apartment and Nick and Nancy's on Henry Street. Joe said, "And would you ask the girl next door to keep feeding the damn cats?" He gave Dave the car keys. "It's a good thing I had the snow tires put on the other day," he said. "I'm rather proud of myself."

There was a public phone just down the hall from the cafeteria, and Simon used it to call school, to say that he wouldn't be coming in. He asked for Mr. Anderson, the headmaster. After Dave explained what had happened, Mr. Anderson said something about hoping that things would be all right, and Dave felt so grateful that tears filled his eyes.

II

THERE WAS A LONG silence as Dave and Louise maneuvered through the heavy traffic at the approach to the Brooklyn Bridge. The traffic stopped entirely halfway across the bridge. Manhattan loomed ahead in the mist like a vast, floating fortress. Dave recalled to himself an incident from his childhood in which Nick had offered to beat up some kid who had called him a kike. "Now I guess I'm talking about him the way you were last night," Dave said out loud. He looked over at Louise and saw that she was fast asleep, her head back on the top of the seat, her thick hair falling away from her face like some heavy, fine cloth. He reached across her and took her right hand, which was hanging down beside the seat, and put it on her lap. The traffic started moving again. "The point is," Dave said quietly.

After dropping Louise off, Dave drove to the West Side Highway by a route that took him along Barrow Street, past the house where he had lived the first ten years of his life. It was a fine old brownstone, now divided up into apartments: he could see the mailboxes in the vestibule as he drove by.

The big lawn in front of the house in Palisades was dusted over with snow. The sky was becoming lighter, and occasionally the sun shone through and made the Hudson sparkle. Upstairs in the rambling house, Dave, carrying a small suitcase, moved from one room to another feeling like a thief. He stood in his mother's room, looking at the painting given her by an Ashcan artist to repay a loan thirty years before, at the white tufted bedspread that he himself had sent home from his summer tour of Europe, at the two Navajo rugs, at the cherrywood bureau and dressing table, at the books and magazines on the dressing table—William Maxwell's *The Folded Leaf*, Furbank's *Life of E. M. Forster*, the Wellesley alumnae bulletin—and he thought about the accident of wealth that permitted all this material and emotional refinement, and then about the sophomore's questions of how it was that he was who he was and not someone else, how it had been arranged that it was not he but his brother who now lay near death. Dizziness nearly overcame him, as it had during his mother's first phone call, and he lay down on her bed, the constellation of his family whirling in his head: he was his brother's older brother, his father's father, his mother's husband, his own father.

There were two faint reports from downstairs. Dave wondered for a moment whether someone was knocking on the front door. But then he heard a jumble of small footfalls in the foyer and then on the stairs, like a minuscule stampede, and he knew that the thumps had been the cat door in the basement banging shut twice. The two orange cats came up the stairs and, full of cupboard love, followed Dave to his father's room, in the rear of the house, away from the river, and far enough away from his mother's room to ensure that his snoring would not disturb her. It was like a rooming-house room, with brown linoleum on the floor, a camp bed, and a functional desk and chair. The clock on the bed table was an old electric one made of yellowing plastic with a large crack in the casing. The shoes in a neat row on the floor under the bed were mostly castoffs from Dave that his father had had fixed and then saddle-soaped and polished. Dave went into the bathroom to get his father's toothbrush. There were cobwebs in the corners where the walls met the ceiling.

He walked toward the front of the house again, past Nick's old room, the cats still trailing him. He went downstairs to give them something to eat. On the door to his own bedroom, next to his brother's, was a sign that said "NO MOLESTE, POR FAVOR," which his father had brought back from a hotel in Argentina a long, long time before. Dave obeyed it, leaving undisturbed the shade of the teen-age boy who retreated there so often to escape his brother's ridicule, who so often at night lay sleepless on the narrow bed, who did not know whether he was hero or scoundrel, dirty or clean, weak or tough, smart or devious, who did not even know, because there was no one with the time or inclination to tell him, whether these doubts were unique or vulgar, inborn or reactionary, and who hoarded them like a miser, because they made him feel special, and because he felt that he would be loved to the degree that he caused no trouble. The bright sun in the kitchen cheered him, and he didn't notice the cold as he walked across the driveway and through a gap in the hedge, toward the neighbors' house, to extend the arrangement for feeding the cats.

Back at his parents' house, he picked up the suitcase he had packed. The cats were lying in a large pool of sunlight on the kitchen counter, washing themselves. Dave realized that he was hungry and looked in the refrigerator. He found a half-empty pint of milk, a stick of margarine with toast crumbs embedded in one of its ends, a half pound of bacon ends and scraps, a can of sauerkraut juice, a bowl with two desiccated chicken wings in it, a jar of rock-solid grated cheese, a frozen-orange-juice can with bacon grease in it, two wrinkled green apples, three eggs, mayonnaise, two flashlight batteries, a bunch of brown carrots with wilted tops, mustard, horseradish, relish, a slice of onion wrapped in aluminum foil, a wine bottle with less than an inch of wine in it, three slices of protein bread in a plastic bag, and a wedge of moldy Cheddar cheese. He wondered idly whether he would someday have children of his own, and whether after they had left home the contents of his refrigerator would be like this, and these speculations made him realize that his life and life in general would continue no matter what happened to his brother. He decided he would have something to eat when he got to the city.

III

NICK WENT INTO A coma for four days. He did not wake or move—except to be turned to avoid bedsores—or, as far as anyone knew, dream or think, or in any other clear way seem to traffic with the numberless fine and gross alterations that create time. Because Nick was between life and death, between time and no-time, more nearly an object in time than a subject of it, and because he was the sole focus of Dave's life, the four days were, for Dave, less like days than space or volume, a physical structure inhabited as a house is inhabited, the days like suites, the hours like rooms, the minutes like the air in those rooms. He would take a turn at sleeping in the apartment across from the hospital and waken not knowing whether it was day or night. He ate breakfast at seven-thirty at night and lunch after midnight. In the morning or evening, he would look out a window at the street in front of the hospital and be momentarily baffled by the surge of cars he saw there, and then he would think, Oh, yes—it must be rush hour. Newspapers mystified him, as if they were dispatches from some other universe.

He was in a dance, a sort of minuet with his mother and father and Louise and Nancy, with Nick at the still center of the circle. He went out for a walk with his mother one cold, clear afternoon. Emily said, "You know, I just had a small argument with Nancy. They want only one of us sitting with Nicky at a time, and Nancy and I were both planning to go in, and she actually said, 'I have more right than you do.' I wanted to say, 'But he's my son.'" Dave said, "She's just upset." Later that day, he was sitting in the lounge with his father. Joe said, "I'm worried about your mother. We had breakfast in the cafeteria this morning, and she had almost no appetite at all. Even in the worst emergency, that woman will eat a healthy meal." Dave said, "She'll be all right. Everybody sleeps—I mean eats too much anyway." He had to reassure Louise that she belonged with the family, that she wasn't in the way, and he listened while Nancy told him that Nick could hardly stand the pressure and competitiveness at his law firm, and envied Dave the more relaxed life of a teacher. Dave knew that he was being talked about, too—that the others, in various pairs and combinations, and always with Nick at the heart of their concern, were weaving him into the web of words with which they were all trying to catch and hold him.

It was agreed that if Nick took any sort of turn, for the better or for the worse, whoever was in the hospital at the time would call the apartment across the street or go over to it, to tell whoever was resting there what had happened. Dave and Louise were sleeping there one afternoon when the door bell rang. Dave, who had been sleeping in his clothes, rushed to the door and opened it. A stranger stood there—a very short, dark-haired woman holding what looked like an oversized briefcase. "Avon calling," she said. Dave said, "We don't want anything, but I can't tell you how happy I am that it's you."

Not long after that, Nick's kidneys shut down completely. In the lounge, the tall resident explained to the family, in his formal way, how dangerous this development was, and said that he and the surgeon and a consulting doctor on the case thought that they should start Nick on peritoneal dialysis, to remove the poisons that had begun to accumulate in his blood.

By late that night, the dialysis had cleared Nick's blood enough to bring him near consciousness. Dave stood in the doorway of the room with his father and Louise and watched while Emily and Nancy loudly called Nick's name and implored him to wake up. Nick moved his head back and forth, and then opened his eyes for a second and smiled faintly, almost mischievously, as if he knew some wonderful secret he wanted to tease them with but not tell them. He closed his eyes again, and the resident, who was also in the room, stepped forward—eagerly, like an ungainly girl who has wanted to dance all night and has finally been asked—checked Nick's pulse and pupils, and said that he was in something more nearly like real sleep than a coma. He shooed everyone except the private nurse out, and they all tiptoed away, smiling. Dave took Louise's hand. She began to cry, and they stopped so that the others would go ahead. "I'm sorry," she said. "It's just such a relief."

The resident came up behind Dave and drew him away. "I wanted to say that although we have an improvement, it may be a temporary result of the dialysis. It's not clear that this is the beginning of a recovery."

"But you're more hopeful?" Dave said.

"Well, yes, but it's not entirely, um, rational. Anything can happen."

"O.K., thank you," Dave said. "Listen, I also want to thank

you for your help in all of this. I don't know what your regular duties are, what your assignment is, but I do know that you've spent more than the normal amount of time and effort with my brother."

"It's an unusual case," the resident said.

"It's not just that. That's the kind of thing that I would say, but I know it's more than that, and I'm grateful for your concern."

In the lounge, everyone chatted cheerfully for a while. Then Nancy and Emily said they wanted to try to get some sleep. "If you're not too exhausted to stay here, my lamb," Emily said to Dave.

"No, I feel fine," Dave said. "You go on. Joe, you go too."

Dave and Louise slept on the couches for a few hours. Just before dawn, Dave dreamed that he was his brother, and that someone was trying to rouse him from a deep sleep. He awoke to find Nick's private-duty nurse gently shaking his shoulder. He said, "Where's Dave?"

"You're Dave, aren't you?" the nurse said.

"Yes. I'm sorry. I guess I was dreaming."

"Well, excuse me for disturbing you, but your brother's awake and he asked to see you."

"Is he all right?" Dave asked as he stood up from the couch. Louise was awake, too.

"He seems to be quite alert," the nurse said.

"I'll call my parents," Dave said.

"But he asked to see you."

"You go on, Davey," Louise said sleepily. "He just wants to see you."

Dave followed the nurse to Nick's room. She let him go in alone. He walked in and stood at the foot of the bed. Nick's head and shoulders were propped up on some pillows.

"I think that was almost the ballgame," Nick said weakly. "How long was I out?"

"A few days. It wasn't the ballgame, though, so don't worry."

"Where are Joe and Em?"

"Over at the apartment with Nancy. They're sleeping."

"Our apartment?"

"Oh, no, that's right, you couldn't have known, what with all your malingering," Dave said. "There's a nurses' and residents' residence"—he gestured with one hand, to acknowledge the repetition—"and we've all been taking care—taking turns sleeping there."

"Why don't you sit down, my young scholar? You look like a tombstone standing there."

Dave went around the bed and sat in the chair next to the head. He leaned forward, put his hands between his knees, curved his shoulders in and held his arms tight against his sides, like a child learning to dive.

"What do the doctors say?"

"Your kidneys weren't working too well, and that's one reason you were unconscious for so long. Urea or uric acid. I forget which it is. Maybe both. They built up in your blood, so they put you on this abdominal dialysis, and that cleared your blood up and you woke up. You're going to be fine now. You really had us scared."

"I'm still incredibly tired, but for some reason I'm not so scared myself now. Is the infection better?"

"You wouldn't be awake if it weren't better," Dave said.

"How's Nancy?" Nick asked.

"Fine. We're all O.K."

"Christ, my arm aches," Nick said.

"It's from the intravenous needles."

"Suddenly I feel just terrible again."

"Well, you don't look bad at all, considering. The nurse shaved you yesterday, and your color isn't bad."

"You're supposed to be sick," Nick said.

"I'm better. A resident gave me a shot of penicillin."

"But are you cold?" Nick said. "You look all hunched up."

"No, I'm fine," Dave said. He took his hands from between his knees and sat back in the chair. He managed to relax a little, but only by an effort of will.

"I feel like I can't really get my breath," Nick said.

"Do you want the nurse?"

"What's she going to do—breathe for me?"

"I'm sorry. I thought she might be able to help. Or the doctor."

"Sorry, Davey. It's just that I feel so crummy."

"Forget it."

Nicholas closed his eyes. Dave sat forward, and then began to get up from the chair. Nicholas waved his right hand feebly. "I'm O.K.," he said. "Just resting. Stick around."

Dave sat down. The room was quiet. He looked at his brother. He thought, If I had to and if there were some way of doing it, I would give my life for his. At first, although he had not the slightest doubt that it was true, the thought astonished him. It was like an arrow that had been shot into him from a distance so great that the archer could not be seen. But then he realized that it had been in him somewhere from the very moment his mother had called him at school, and that he had felt as though he were its quarry, and now that it had tracked him down here and cornered him, and he had turned at last to face it, he saw that it was not alien, but part of himself.

The room was filled with a kind of pewter light. Nothing moved. It was as though the pendulum of every clock in the world had stopped for a moment at the top of its arc. Nick opened his eyes and smiled. "Is Joe all right?" he asked, but his eyes seemed to be asking some other question. He turned his head toward the door and said, with a tone of genuine curiosity, "Who's that?"

"There's no one there, Nicky."

Nicholas turned his face back toward Dave. He said, firmly, "Davey, this is it." He took a deep breath, like someone who is about to swim down to the bottom of a lake to find something valuable he has lost there, and then he died.

Dave became aware of the hissing of the heating vent behind him. He turned and saw that the curtain hanging over it was moving slightly. He stood up and closed his brother's eyes, and then he sat down again and cried.

IV

NANCY WENT TO THE apartment on Henry Street by taxi. She would get her car and drive up to Palisades later in the day. Louise and Dave sat in the back seat of Joe's car. Joe drove and Emily sat in front. As they made their way out of the parking lot, the sun, just above the horizon, caught a window in the hospital and set it ablaze. Joe stopped the car before pulling out onto the avenue. He said, "Davey, which—"

"You go left here, Joe," Dave said.

I Spy

IN THE THIRTIES AND forties, my father belonged to the Communist Party. They sent him to Mexico, to keep an eye on Trotsky in exile. As he tells it, he got to be friends with one of Trotsky's bodyguards, and liked him so much that when he got back to New York he deliberately falsified his report. My father also knew Russian agents and Americans working for Russia, but he says he had no part in the espionage. My father likes to talk about how much more active he was as a radical than his brother, my Uncle Sol, who nowadays makes a much bigger thing of his politics than my father does. My mother says she went along with my father's revolutionary aspirations because she was so in love with him. They both had regular and unlikely jobs—she as a proofreader for the *Wall Street Journal* and he as an institutional-insurance salesman. My mother once told me that in 1946 she was crossing a busy intersection with a friend of my father's who was supposedly some sort of salesman, and he said to her, "You know, Emily, if a car were to hit me or something like that, for your own good you must keep on walking and pretend to have no idea who I am."

I Spy

In those days, when I was in grade school and we lived in the Village, on Barrow Street, different pairs of extremely neat men wearing striped suits and well-blocked hats would show up at our apartment. In the living room, behind two tall sliding doors that rumbled like thunder in their tracks and met in the middle of the floor with what seemed to a child like dreadful finality, the men would have long talks with my father. "They are from the government, Davey," my mother would say. "They need your father to help them." I could hear the strain in her voice as clearly as I could see it in the smiles of the two neat men.

Once, one of the men stayed behind when his pal left. He was immensely tall—six-four, as it turned out—and I was sure he was going to get me behind those sliding doors and kill me. Instead, he took off his coat, revealing a shoulder holster with a huge blue-black gun nestled in it. He draped his coat over the piano, unbuckled the holster, and held the gun in front of my astonished eyes, saying, as if from the top of a mountain, "What do you think of that?" He then sat down and had a cup of coffee with my parents.

This was Jim McCray. A year after Jim stayed behind and bowled me over with the sight of that monstrous pistol, my mother told me that he, and not my Uncle Sol, would be my guardian if anything ever happened to her and my father. I was hazy about what that meant, but hearing it made me feel happy and safe. That Jim became a close friend of my family's was an odd turn of events but not entirely surprising. During the conversation behind closed doors, my father and Jim discovered that they had both been born in Perth Amboy in the same year and for nearly a decade had lived only a few blocks apart. Anyway, my father has always been able to strike up friendships in the most unlikely situations.

Jim helped to keep my father and my Uncle Sol out of trouble with the F.B.I. and HUAC in the early fifties, and when he left the Bureau to become head of corporate security for Worldwide

Products he stayed close to us. He's retired now. He and his wife live near my parents, up in Rockland County, in Nyack, and they see one another all the time. As for me, I live on Riverside Drive with my wife, Elizabeth. After a couple of years of teaching English in prep school, a year as a reporter for a now extinct West Side weekly newspaper, and five years of covering City Hall for the *Times*, I got tired of all the petty politics and skulduggery and took a job as a professor at Columbia Journalism School, which is what I do now. Classes were over a few days ago. Elizabeth and I will spend a lot of time up at our rented summer place, in Rhinebeck, and I may try a free-lance piece or two for the *Times Magazine*, but I have no regular work to do for the first time since the summer I was twenty-one and went to see Jim McCray about a job.

It was in 1963. Just as I was about to finish my senior year at Haverford and go to work as a copyboy for the Rockland County *Journal-News*, the job fell through. I hadn't been home in Nyack for more than a week, looking desultorily for work, when Jim called me up and asked me to come down to Worldwide Products headquarters, in Englewood Cliffs, to talk something over with him. "It would be better not to discuss this on the phone," he said, and my first thought was that it might have something to do with my father.

The Worldwide Products Company building was set back from Route 9-W like a fort. It was modern, low-slung, and rambling, and all you could see of it from the road was a flash of reflected sunlight from one of the smoked-glass windows or a glimpse of white marble. Jim's office jutted out from the back of the building, and the trees that crowded around his three big pearl-gray windows made me feel as if I were in some kind of natural stockade. Jim himself looked the same then, at fifty-five, as he does now— iron-gray hair, a white mustache, eyes as blue as poker chips.

His voice was high and sweet but dignified. If you asked him to show you the scar from a bullet wound on his right arm, which he got in a car chase that saw the end of some famous Depression-era criminal's wild career, in 1942, he'd roll up his sleeve and say, "Oh, that. That's nothing—just a stray shot. . . . The amazing thing was that some pal of the fugitive had called him the night before and told him we had found out where he was hiding, but he thought that this fella, who was a notorious drinker and practical joker, was pulling his leg."

When I asked Jim if there was some trouble about my father, he said, "Oh, no, don't worry, don't worry; this has nothing to do with your dad."

We sat down on opposite sides of his mesa-sized glass desk. "That's all over and done with," Jim said. "He never knew very much anyway, to tell you the truth. No sense in their picking on him. But I do hope you won't mention anything to him about my little proposition. I know how he feels about big corporations and their shenanigans."

"O.K.," I said, with a pang of an unfamiliar kind of guilt.

"I'd like you to go out to the Midwest and do a little informal spying for us," Jim said.

"Spying?"

"Nothing illegal, nothing illegal—don't worry about that. The Murchison Company has a big new plant out in East St. Louis, Illinois, and we're afraid that they may be making a new type of instant iced tea in it. Our product-development people are pretty worried, because we're working on the same thing, and we want to be first on the market. I'll pay you two hundred and fifty dollars, plus expenses, to go out there for a week and snoop around a little—find out if they're working on this stuff, how far along they are, and so forth. It's illegal to go onto the factory's property for espionage purposes, but just about anything else is fair game. What do you think?"

"It sounds like fun," I said, thinking how strange it was that grown men and women were going home at night and sitting at the kitchen table with a half-empty bottle of liquor in front of them, worrying about a race between two brands of instant iced tea.

"I don't think this will be fun," Jim said. "But I thought it might interest you, since you want to be a reporter. Now, are you sure that doing this sort of work won't bother you?"

"Bother me?"

"Well, you're a sensitive young fella, and . . ."

"I'd like to give it a try," I said.

"That's the ticket, Davey me boy." Jim opened a desk drawer, took out an envelope, and handed it to me. "Count it," he said. There were ten fifty-dollar bills. "Now let me tell you more about what's involved."

"What will you be doing in St. Louis, Mr. Leonard?" asked the pretty girl sitting next to me on the plane, after we had introduced ourselves. She was going home to St. Louis from nursing school in the East, and she spoke with a Southern drawl. I had never known that Missourians could have a drawl. I had also never flown before, and I had never been west of the Poconos.

"Well, I'm in law school at Penn, and I've got a job as a clerk for a judge in St. Louis," I said.

"Really?" she said. "My father's a lawyer. Which judge will you be working for?"

"Justice . . . um, Blarney."

"I don't believe I've ever heard that name," she said.

"He's new. He's one of those Irishmen, but he looks like me. A real coincidence. He's older than I am. Of course. But he's got wavy brown hair, about six feet tall, too skinny. Ha, ha."

"How interesting," she said. "And where will you be living?"

"In the southern part of the city. You know, south St. Louis.

I forget the name of the street. I'm supposed to call this person when I get off the plane." There was a long pause. "He has diabetes—the judge, I mean. Listen, maybe you can tell me what diabetes actually is."

At the St. Louis airport I rented a car. I got lost in the city for a while, but I finally found the bridge over the Mississippi to Granite City and East St. Louis. There I got lost once again, and found myself driving past gigantic factories with tall, blank walls, like cliff faces: East City Steel Company, United Starch & Refining Company, American Lead, Hubell Metals, Slattery Tar & Chemical, Wesco Steel Barrel, Illinois Fire Brick, East Shore Slag. Rows and rows of three-story attached houses and listing, flaking asbestos-sided cottages in time-dimmed shades of blue, yellow, green, and red. It was an amazing and disillusioning thing for me to travel through the heart of the kind of place I'd only caught a glimpse or a whiff of from the Garden State Parkway and the New Jersey Turnpike.

The Murchison plant occupied two blocks on the north side of Jefferson Street. Directly opposite it was a bar and a bunch of dilapidated wooden bungalows. East of the bungalows sat a brick parochial school a block long whose playground, behind a high chain-link fence, consisted of a broad patch of dirt fringed by tufts of crabgrass. Then another block of bungalows, and then the motel that I stayed in. It was a yellow stucco barrackslike building, and its name was as blunt as everything else about East St. Louis seemed to be: Bob's Motel. I checked in at three o'clock, just in time to watch a long stream of children pass the window of my room. The boys all wore white shirts, green jackets, and green shorts, and the girls had on green skirts and white blouses. "Why do you wanna ..." "... saw the biggest ..." "... three doubles and a homer ..." "... Mary Ellen said she ..." "... got sick, and he's a dumb ..." "... sock him as hard as ..." Their voices rang out and then died away, leaving the street hot, empty, and silent, except for the thin sound of some country music drifting along like an old dog's leash trailing in the dust.

I put through a call to Jim. "Well, I'm here," I said. "The plant is just up the street, and I've got a terrific view of it and the loading bays and the railway spur that runs through the yard. Do you think I should—"

"Are you in the motel right now?" Jim said.

"Yes, I just got—"

"Don't talk there, don't talk there. I should have told you. Find a phone booth."

"You mean someone might—"

"Find a phone booth and call me back collect."

I went outside and walked farther east, and in looking down the street for a public telephone I caught sight of the children far ahead, dancing in the sun like leaves.

"The fella at the desk might be a little bored and listen in," Jim said when I called him back. "You've got to think about these things, me lad."

"Right," I said. "I'm sorry."

"Well, what's the trouble?"

"Nothing. I just thought you might like to know that I arrived safe and sound. Renting the car was a snap, and everything went fine." Then, though I didn't want to, I added, "This is some depressing place."

"You'll get used to it, you'll get used to it. You don't have to call again unless there's some emergency."

Parts of the new Murchison plant were already in operation, but its construction hadn't been completed. The factory consisted of three tan blocklike buildings of different sizes grouped around a concrete tower. West of the tower another block was going up, its dull-red girders poking into the air like blasted, limbless saplings. On top of the tower sat a big black wedge-shaped structure, and out of that wedge, for four or five hours every day, came the whitest of white steam, accompanied by a great rushing, hissing sound. The top of the tower was lit up at night, and when the steam was vented after dark, it looked luminescent, almost ethereal, as if the spirit of whatever was being made down below had been discarded and sent heavenward. Sometimes the plant worked on one eight-hour shift per day, sometimes two, and sometimes three, and sometimes it was on what appeared to be half shifts. The blue-coverall-clad workmen advanced on the building and receded from it like small waves lapping at a titanic sand castle. During the daytime, trucks of all kinds pulled up to the loading docks and later pulled away again; less often, trains hauling three or four freight cars would crawl slowly up or down the railway spur that ran east of the plant and seemed to end somewhere behind it. In a notebook I drew pictures of the plant and kept a record of the shifts, the venting times and durations, and the names on the sides of the trucks—Columbia Containerizing, Plastiseal, Glassco, White Star Sugar, Midwest Pneumatic.

I walked up and down the street again and again, so that I could see the trucks' license plates and check how tight security was at the gate, which I couldn't see from the motel, and I stared at the factory from my window for hours on end. The staring had no practical purpose; it was as if I were enchanted. At night, I used my alarm clock to wake me every hour, so that I could record whether and when operations shut down. Those semiconscious interludes were ghostly, almost hallucinatory, especially when the plant was running and those great clouds of steam were issuing from it.

"He knows what you're up to," said a voice from the barstool on my right. It was five o'clock on Tuesday, and I was in the Cardinal Bar and Grill, across from the factory; about twenty workers from the day shift had come in for a beer.

"I'm sorry, were you talking to me?" I said, trying to keep

the alarm out of my voice. The man sitting to my right was short and cherubic, with red cheeks and a tonsure-like fringe of gray hair. He had on a blue plant uniform, and he was drinking a Coke.

"He knows everything you think and everything you do," the man said.

"Who does?"

"Why, God does, son. He knoweth every time you tell a lie, and He remembereth it, too. Do you walk with Him?"

"Well, I guess I'm not all that religious," I said, and tried to swivel back around and face the bar.

The cherub pushed me gently on the shoulder. "But God loveth you," he said.

"Why don't you leave this poor boy alone?" said a huge, sallow man who was resting his belly against the bar just beyond where the cherub was sitting. "Don't pay any attention to Hallie here, son. His wife left him four years ago and he got religion instead of getting around, which is what any sane man would do—ain't that right, Jimmy?" He reached out and fondled the chest of another man in blue who was walking by.

"Whatever you say, Grady," the man said as he walked on.

"Give this boy a drink," Grady said to the bartender. "What are you drinking, son—beer or beer?"

"I guess I'll have a beer," I said.

"That would be about right. I didn't catch your name."

"It's Dave."

"Grady."

"I know."

"Too big a target to miss, huh?"

The beers came. Hallie, muttering something about sin, got up and walked away, and Grady sat down. "I know you don't work over at the plant," he said.

"No, that's right. I'm sort of visiting. I'm not from around here."

"I could tell that from the way you talk. If there's something in the way of sightseeing in this town, I don't know about it."

"I'm not sightseeing," I said. "I'm trying to get to see my girlfriend."

"The women," Grady said.

"She's not the trouble; her father is."

"I can mind my own business."

"Oh, that's O.K.," I said. "See, we went to school together in Pennsylvania. We were going to get married this summer, but her father stepped in."

"School?"

"Well, college. Her father is a vice-president at United Starch, and they live just out of town, in Ladue. I'm trying to get to see her."

"You seem all right to me, though you might be a bit on the skinny side."

"It's because I'm Jewish," I said.

"Well, hell, Dave, that don't make no difference."

"To him it does."

"I could see it if you was of the Negro persuasion."

"You know, if I have to stay around here, I'm going to run out of money," I said. "Do you think the factory could use anyone part time for a few weeks?"

"They got a personnel office. You don't have to tell no one it's just for a while."

"I know it's the Murchison Company, but I don't even know what they're making."

"Just go on up to the gate and ask for the personnel office."

"Well, maybe I will," I said. "Let me buy you back that beer."

"Hey, Grady, you want to try a game or two?" called a man standing next to the bowling machine by the door.

"Get yourself a partner," Grady yelled back. "That's my cousin Andy, Dave. You can tell from his waistline. Can you use that machine?"

"I'm pretty good at it," I said. "Though it depends on the machine."

"We'll pin his ears back for him."

Grady had to lift his belly over the edge of the board before he could slide the puck down the alley, and he had a way of reaching over the foul line which caused a lot of good-natured complaints. "House rules," he would say. He and the men we played against grumbled about someone named Johnston at the plant—I guessed he was their foreman—but it was mostly wives and baseball and cars. And racism—of a kind at once so casual and so virulent that at the time I couldn't believe that these men, who otherwise seemed decent, had their whole heart in what they were saying. Grady eventually left, and I got a hamburger and some French fries from the grill in the back and sat at the bar for another hour, but I didn't learn a thing.

Sta-Fast Labels, Missouri license plates; Red Diamond Hauling, Ohio; Occidental Office Supplies, Indiana; Little Rock Ink & Dye, Arkansas. Two trains a day, marked either "Soo Line" or "Illinois Central." Two shifts Tuesday, one Wednesday, two and a half Thursday. Falling asleep in the chair in front of the window in my motel room, dreaming of drowning under a waterfall, awakening at three-thirty in the morning to find the steam pouring from the top of the plant as if the whole thing were an upside-down rocket boring into the earth. "She called me when her father was at work and said maybe we could meet somewhere this weekend." "Let me buy you a beer." "You and Grady work at the same job over there?" "Andy here swears he'll never be married." "I'd love to beat you, Grady, but my wife will have my hair if I don't get home." Shouts from the children in the dusty playground at recess, the drone of recitation floating out the school's windows and down the street, borne by a hot, oppressive breeze.

On Thursday evening, at the bar, I asked Grady's cousin what the plant was making, and he said, "How come you're so interested?"

"Well, I figured that if I'm going to ask for a job over there, I'd like to know what I'd be doing."

"This kind of job's just a job," he said. "It don't matter what you're doing. If you need the money, why don't you do something about it instead of sitting here jawing? You don't want no job here."

I had already begun to get the feeling that some of the other men had become suspicious about me, so I left as quickly and inconspicuously as I could.

On Friday, as I was walking past the school at recess, one of the teachers on the playground beckoned me over to the fence. "Sonny, I don't know why you would want to walk along here all the time," she said. "But you had better just stay away from these children."

That night, at seven, I locked the door to my room and walked down to the public phone and called Jim at home.

"Listen, I've had about as much of this as I can handle," I said.

"Is anyone on to you? Are they asking questions?" He sounded less concerned than excited, like a child in the midst of anticipation.

"A little," I said. "But it's not that. The whole thing makes me uneasy."

"Well, it's just two more days. I sure would like to know whether that plant operates on Sunday. Just lie low, keep your eye on the place. See if you can get into some conversations."

"But I've been doing all that," I said. "You certainly were right about one thing—it isn't fun."

"It just takes patience. That's the key. We really would like to know what's going on out there. Hang on. See if you can get into some conversations. And come in to see me on Monday, when you get back."

At the motel, a man was leaning against the door to my room. He was swarthy and wiry, and was dressed in a sweat-stained blue shirt and khakis.

"Are you the guy who's supposed to be looking for work?" he asked.

"Yes, I'm out here trying to see my girlfriend," I said. "My money's just about to—"

"Andy Thaxton told me about you. My name's Johnston. What's yours?"

"Dave. David."

"You're as phony as a snake's leg," he said, crossing his arms. "What do you want out here?"

"I told you—just a job. My girlfriend's old man—"

"Girlfriend my ass. Why don't you clear out of here before you get yourself into some real trouble? You're just about old enough to wear a jock, ain't you? How come they sent a kid like you?"

"It's the truth. Andy, Grady knows—"

"If you was just a little older, I'd call the cops."

"I haven't broken any laws," I said.

He pushed himself off the door and cuffed the side of my head so hard that tears came to my eyes. "Don't talk laws to me, boy. Just clear on out."

As I watched Johnston walk away, I had the most peculiar impulse to follow him. I wanted to apologize to him, to explain things to him, to have him put his arm around my shoulders and invite me home for a beer. I wanted to work at the factory, to put on those blue coveralls every morning, to live in that place, so that I would be able to look twice at strangers. I wanted to go over to the Cardinal at quitting time and complain about the niggers down in Selma. I wanted to consider with envy the rich men who lived in the fancy suburbs of St. Louis.

. . .

My father has always known that I once did some work for Jim. That much I told him. Over the years, he has asked me from time to time exactly what the job was. When I wouldn't tell him, he would laugh as if we were partners in some hilarious crime, as if my not telling him told him something else about me—something he approved of. He's getting old now, though, and yesterday, when I was driving him up to Nyack after picking him up at the dentist's, on Seventy-second Street, we got stuck in a traffic jam on West End Avenue, and, looking for something to talk about, I finally spilled the beans. What harm could it do now, and anyway we've been telling each other a lot of secrets lately; I guess we both know that the time for secrets is growing shorter.

When I finished the story, he said, "I guessed it was something like that. Was the information you got of any use to Jim?"

"I don't know," I said. "I typed it all up and gave it to him on that Monday. He said it was a good job and that they might be able to get some kind of pattern from my notes. He also said that the men not talking and the stuff with Johnston probably meant something secret was going on. But I think he was disappointed. He couldn't blame me for leaving right away, but I could tell that he was hoping I'd get the goods on that plant. I thought he was more disappointed about *my* not getting the goods than about not getting the goods, if you know what I mean."

"Ouch!" my father said. "That bastard really did a job yanking my tooth out. The Novocain's beginning to wear off."

"I wasn't really cut out for that kind of work," I said. "The ironic thing is that Worldwide did get their tea on the market first but it wasn't as good as the Murchison stuff."

"I know," my father said. "I use the Murchison myself. But don't tell Jim."

Just then the traffic cleared a little, and we drove on. We hit a red light at 100th Street and stopped right beside the Strathmore, an old hotel that has just been renovated.

"My God, look at the Strathmore," my father said. "What a coincidence! That's where all the spies lived."

"Russian or American?" I said.

"A lot of times, you couldn't tell. Everybody was spying on everybody. Sometimes it got to be very funny. And, you know, that's where I first laid eyes on Jim McCray. I was visiting someone in the hotel, and when I came out, why, I caught sight of this tall fellow standing across the street, leaning against a car. He was trying to look nonchalant, but he was so obviously an F.B.I. man that it was ridiculous. He tailed me into the subway, but I lost him at Columbus Circle. It was an old trick. A few weeks later he came calling on us at Barrow Street."

"I never knew he was watching you," I said.

"It's a fact. Those days seem romantic to me now, but at the time it was boring and silly. And a lot more dangerous than I realized. I guess I wasn't very good at it, either."

"But if they were all spies, why did they all live together in the same hotel?" I asked as the light turned green.

"They were lonely," my father said.

Interference

ON A BEAUTIFUL SUNDAY evening at the end of June, Elizabeth and I stopped at Uncle Sol's farmhouse overnight. We were on our way from New York to the small cottage in Vermont we had rented sight unseen for the first three weeks in July. At about seven-thirty, we got to the top of Two-Mile Hill, outside Sheffield, where you turn off Route 24 onto Route 58 for the last couple of miles to Uncle Sol's place. I said to Elizabeth, "Why don't you take the bike off the rack and ride it the rest of the way? Then it will be a double surprise—first me showing up unexpectedly and then you. He loves stuff like that." Elizabeth was, of course, reluctant—as she always is about what she calls my "stunts," and about being forced into the center of attention, as she would be when she straggled up the driveway at Uncle Sol's five minutes or so after I got there. So I said it would give her a chance to try out the bike, which was very new, very blue and shiny, and she seemed to find that argument persuasive, though I think that, again as usual, she was warming a little to the idea of being forced into the center of attention. We stopped and got the bike down, I told her which house it was, and off I went.

As I reached the crest of the small hill above Uncle Sol's and saw the huge red barn, the neat white-trimmed red farmhouse, and the vegetable garden between them, I said to myself what Uncle Sol always said when as a kid I would ride back from town with him: "I wonder who lives in that beautiful red house. I understand it's a funny-looking short gentleman in his sixties who never got married. Nope, he never got married, though he had plenty of chances. And he has the most *peculiar* relatives, including a young fellow named David who claims to be his nephew but who is actually, they tell me, the Prince of Wales. Yes, the Jewish Prince of Wales visits the old man every summer, and every night they eat bean soup and belly buttons." This tale I found hysterically funny, but, then, I have never minded being the center of anyone's attention. As I got older, my response to it went through several changes. Four years old (giggling): "No, *we* live there, *we* live there." Eight: "And the old man is bald and has big ears and a big nose. He is the King of Wales and"—shouting—"his face looks like an elephant." Twelve: "Unfortunately, the old man is so chintzy he forgot to buy the Prince some ice cream." Sixteen (my last full summer up there; I'm at the wheel): "It's the Prince who has the peculiar relatives, if you ask me."

When I pulled up the driveway Sunday, without Elizabeth, everything looked more or less as it should: Uncle Sol's old station wagon parked halfway in the garage on the left; the horse barn in front of me, its only inhabitant for nearly forty years a Ping-Pong table; and the lawn and flower gardens sloping up the hill between the horse barn and the house. But one of the station wagon's rear tires was flat, the paint on the barn's white sliding door was peeling, the gardens were a salad of weeds and legitimate flowers, and the house looked generally strange. It was still in fairly good shape. In the company of Uncle Sol's usual July-and-August coterie of cousins, visiting Communists, unemployed college-graduate friends of cousins, doctors' sons and daughters from neighboring summer houses, I had painted the place three years before. And I had been giving Uncle Sol a little money from time to time for the past three or four years—ever since I got tenure at Columbia—to have the roof fixed, shore up the foundation, replace some rotting boards on the porch, hire a handyman for a couple of weeks, etc. Conscience money, I called it, to repay him for putting up with me and my older brother, Nick, in the summers long ago while my parents toiled away in the polio-plagued city. But now, with the sun slanting down on it, with the cawing of three glossy crows in the dead elm behind it, and with the brook that runs through the meadow to the south sounding for all the world like the laughter of children heard from a great distance, the house seemed forlorn. The windows were gray, nearly opaque, as if covered for sleep by some nictitation, but I could vaguely make out three heads in the kitchen, gliding past each other, meeting and turning back, tilting forward occasionally as if in prayer.

In the kitchen I found Uncle Sol, eighty-six; my second cousin, Ella, ninety (she's a retired schoolteacher, who lives in the city and spends her summers at Uncle Sol's, paying him what little she can from her pension and Social Security); and my other surviving uncle, Pete, a mere eighty-two. (Like Uncle Sol, Pete worked for a settlement house in New York. He moved to a retirement community in Southern California ten years ago, when his wife died, but he visits the East every summer.)

They had been drying dishes and putting them away, but they all stopped in their tracks when I came in, and they looked at me as if they were hoping for some piece of great good news.

"Well, if it isn't Wynken, Blynken, and Nod," I said.

"*You,*" said Uncle Sol, smacking his forehead with the heel of his hand, like a Ukrainian peasant. "You little sneak."

"Hello there, Mister," said Ella, stepping forward with great dignity to receive my kiss on the cheek. Her shoulders were like doorknobs under my hands. She stepped back and put her hand behind her right ear. From it came two shrill squeaks and a modulation down a few notes to a longer, louder whistle. She swatted at the side of her head, at the small bird that seemed to have got fouled in her lovely white hair, and the whistling stopped.

Uncle Sol said, "That's it—give it a good kick."

Pete said, "Why, David, the prodigal nephew. What a surprise. I thought you and Elaine had left for Maine yesterday."

"It's Elizabeth," I said, "and we're taking a few weeks in Vermont, not Maine. She's got some work to catch up on, so she's going by bus the middle of next week."

"A likely story," Uncle Sol said, putting away a glass that looked as though it had been washed in Wildroot. "I bet she thinks she's too good for the likes of us."

"That's right," I said. "She doesn't associate with anyone under five-six, which leaves all three of you out."

"Such a sense of humor," Uncle Sol said. "Who taught you to be such a smart-aleck?"

"My father," I said.

"Your father, your father. I taught you everything you know, Vercingetorix. J'eat?"

"Something on the road."

"He had a dead squirrel," Uncle Sol explained to Pete.

"How are your parents?" Joe asked.

"Oh, they're fine," I said. "They send everyone their love."

"How are the folks?" Ella asked as she reached up and gave the skin at the back of my neck a piecrust pinch.

"You can hear him," Uncle Sol said. "She's got a new thingumabob for her hearing," he said to me. "What a difference it has made around here without all the shouting."

"And where is your girlfriend?" Ella said. "I'd like to meet her."

I was now standing in front of the sink, with my back to the window. The three of them were facing me in a line—two hundred and fifty-odd years of one thing or another packed into three wizened, hoary heads. Then their mouths opened and they pointed out toward the driveway, like some ancient rock-and-roll group about to start singing.

"Why, you little sneak," Uncle Sol said. "Playing tricks on your great-great-grandfather." He took a few steps forward and smacked me on top of the head.

"Well, I'll be damned," Pete said, faking a punch at my stomach. "That must be Emily on that bicycle."

Three Mooglike pipings came from Ella's head. "Who's out there?" she said.

"You can hear," Uncle Sol yelled.

Ever since I stopped going to Uncle Sol's for the summer, and especially since my brother died, ten years later, I've dreamed about the place. In some dreams, I rule over it as though it were a feudal fiefdom. In others, I am trying to flee to it for safety from some catastrophe, but my car breaks down or I find the place in ruins when I get there. Sometimes I dream that I am walking around in my apartment in New York only to have it slowly transform itself room by room into Uncle Sol's farmhouse.

My father has always claimed that I should inherit the place. He is old and failing now. He passes many of his days watching Yankee games on television, but I don't think he could name more than two or three of the team's starting lineup. He nods in front of the set with the big orange cat named Debs asleep on his lap. He has claimed that he helped Uncle Sol buy the place forty years ago. He has said that Uncle Sol criticized him for going into business but borrowed from him the very capital he so despised to buy the farm and land. He has said that in the distant past Uncle Sol made a promise to put me up in the summers and to leave the place to him or my mother or me when he died, in return for my father's cancelling the loan. So when I was sixteen, and Uncle Sol told everyone he had decided to leave the house to the Young Communists' League, to start a school based on Socialist principles, my father was furious. My father has also said that in his twenties he was a more serious Communist than Uncle Sol ever was. He has claimed that he was even assigned to play a minor, diversionary role in Trotsky's assassination in Mexico.

But my father has left politics and other passions far behind now. From time to time, he raises a mild complaint about my not being the heir to the farmhouse—he did when Elizabeth and I visited him the night before we went to Uncle Sol's. But his account to her of the transactions and guarantees of half a century ago was a Dickensian jumble of forgotten dates and half-remembered conversations. I was sure there must be truth in what he said, but the whole matter was never in my hands in the first place, and the property has been in my mind so entirely identified with Uncle Sol that I've always felt he ought to do with it as he pleased.

After losing himself and Elizabeth somewhere in the early fifties, my father soon returned to nodding his still handsome gray head in front of the TV while before him young men whose names he didn't know slapped each other on the back or slouched off the field in disappointment. He is drifting farther and farther from everything I know anything about. It breaks my heart to think of him; I wish I could wipe out every unkind word I ever spoke to him, and there were many. I think that he may always have been jealous of Uncle Sol's influence over me, but he needn't worry about that, for I am no one's son but his.

Elizabeth and I started living together last September. We had met six months earlier, in the Hall of Marsupials at the Museum of Natural History. She is assistant curator of the department that deals with those improbable, pocketed creatures, and she marched right up to me and asked, "How do you like my exhibit?" This forwardness was uncharacteristic of her, as I was quickly to learn, but, she told me later, she had liked my curly dark hair and my figure. I'm not sure that I had known until then that men had figures, as such—one of the many things I've learned from her. As for me, I liked her intelligence and her height—six feet even —and the fact that she sometimes breathed through her mouth, like an asthmatic child.

Generally, Elizabeth is shy and reserved, as befits her rural New England background and her Bryn Mawr education, but she has somehow nevertheless managed to get a lot of work done on me. She is determined to make our relationship last, and I have presented her with no mean challenge—a seemingly unreconstructible West Side college-professor bachelor, six years her senior, and Jewish, at that—but she has gone at it like a psychiatrist, roofer, hot-walker, and plumber all rolled into one. This is what she has accomplished on our joint behalf so far: First she persuaded me to let her move into my dingy West End Avenue first-floor steerage apartment, right above the super and his besotted, harridan wife. Four months later, she convinced me that we should move. We bought a co-op overlooking the Hudson on Riverside Drive. And now it seems that we have decided to get married and have children.

The first time Elizabeth met Uncle Sol was in New York. He winters at a public-housing-project apartment on West Seventeenth Street. Elizabeth and I had driven down to his neighborhood one dreary day, early in February, to see my department's research assistant, Jane, who was recuperating from surgery. I'm not too good around sick people, but Jane seemed to be cheered up by the way I kept saying for the hour and a half we were there that we couldn't stay too long.

When we finally left, Elizabeth said, "Doesn't your Uncle Sol live near here?" I said yes. "Do you think this would be a good time for me to meet him?" Before I could answer, she said never mind, she knew he wouldn't like her, but I saw from her expression that she did want to meet him. Then *I* got shy. Maybe some other day would be better, I said. "Well, why don't you just try calling him?" Elizabeth said. "He's probably not home anyway."

Four young black men stood on the steps outside Uncle Sol's project, shivering and drinking from bottles hidden in brown paper bags. A bunch of old ladies sat in the lobby on lawn chairs that they must have brought down from their apartments, clucking with disapproval about the drinkers outside. "You make a very handsome couple," one of the ladies said to Elizabeth after Uncle Sol buzzed us in. Some kids must have been playing rainy-day elevator games, because when we finally got one it stopped at every floor up to the twenty-first.

Uncle Sol and Elizabeth took to each other like two crooks who need each other's skills to bring off some big heist. In the living room Elizabeth said how much she admired Uncle Sol's Mexican rugs, and he told her the one about the first time he went to Mexico and stayed at the house of some leftist friend of his who had a teen-age daughter named Theresa—how when he came down for dinner from the balcony outside his room a little late one evening his host asked him where he had been, and he said, "*Arriba, sobre la teresa*," faking a word for "terrace" and not realizing at first that he had just told the man he'd been upstairs on top of his daughter. Elizabeth laughed and blushed. Then Uncle Sol prodded her a little about her politics, and she was evasively liberal and managed to deflect him. He pressed a week's worth of *Daily World*s on her—"for a different slant on the news," as he put it. "Your friend over there won't read it," he said, pointing at me, "because he's a big-shot journalism professor who knows all the answers." He was thrilled to hear that as a junior at Swarthmore Elizabeth's second cousin, Midge Montgomery, had tried to organize the college's kitchen staff. Then Elizabeth sat down at the ancient, tinny upright piano and played some Methodist hymns and a few songs from one of Uncle Sol's collection of decomposing songbooks—"Tenting on the Old Camp Ground," "Aura Lee," and "A Bicycle Built for Two." When she got up, professing embarrassment over her bad playing, Uncle Sol said, "She's an angel; what I can't figure out is why she took up with you, boy."

Feeling like the third man on the bicycle, I said I had some papers to grade and it was time we got going. Just before we left, Elizabeth astonished me by inviting Uncle Sol to come with us to a Knick game sometime. Even more astonishing, instead of saying something like "You young people and your ath-a-letics," as I expected him to, Uncle Sol replied, "That might be sorta amusing." Then he went on, "If you're interested in sports, young lady, there's a column in one of those newspapers you're stealing from me that you ought to read. It's about the economics of baseball. The profits the owners make are out of this world. It's all part of the same lousy system, and something drastic is about to happen, believe you me. It's got to happen, and it's going to be soon." He has sung this particular refrain more and more often as he has grown older, and I've begun to think that he's actually speaking of his own death without realizing it, so I let it pass. I pretty much stopped arguing with him about politics years ago.

At the door, Uncle Sol said, "I hope you make it up to the house sometime this summer, boy. You'd better take what you want now, because I'm not sure how much longer I'll be around. But don't you dare show up without her."

Elizabeth, not the kissy type but full of spontaneity that day, leaned over and kissed Uncle Sol goodbye. "It was wonderful to meet you," she said. "I can see why David talks about you all the time. I wish I had an interesting family."

"You mean crazy," Uncle Sol said. "Go on, git."

As we walked through the lobby, the same old lady remarked, "Well, if it isn't Their Royal Highnesses." One of the black guys outside panhandled a quarter from me. "It's this lousy system that puts people on the street corner," I said sarcastically as we walked toward the car. "Well, you know, it is," Elizabeth said. I threw the propaganda onto the back seat and we got in.

"Why isn't he leaving the place to you?" Elizabeth asked as we drove up Tenth Avenue.

"Because of his Socialist-school idea—I told you."

"But that's so harebrained. The trouble is, he's afraid of you, because he thinks you have contempt for his politics."

"But he doesn't have any politics, really—that's the trouble."

"And you let him know."

"I don't say a word anymore," I said. "Anyway, it's nothing for you to be concerned about."

"He wishes you were closer to him. And I think you ought to be. And you ought to have that place. Both of you know it, but you're both stubborn."

"Amazing—a single one-hour conversation, a little 'Tea for Two,' and you can tell all that," I said, suddenly feeling extremely resentful of all this interference. "You make it sound so simple. Just step right in and move us to a lovely new apartment and raighten out my family entanglements with a few sentences on Tenth Avenue." I had a clear, happy vision of the door on Elizabeth's side of the car falling off and of her flying out. "What's in this for you, anyway?"

"Why, whatever do you mean?" she said.

That Sunday in June, after introducing Elizabeth to Ella and Pete (Ella: "Well, Miss, it's about time I got a look at you"; Pete: "My gosh, you're a tall one"), I took her on a tour of Uncle Sol's while it was still light. When we got back to the house, we found the three musketeers in the living room, Uncle Sol with his back to us, just starting a game of Scrabble on the long pine table in front of the fireplace. " 'Jo,' " Uncle Sol was saying. "It's a perfectly good word, Ella—you know that. It means 'sweetheart' in Scottish dialect—'My Johnny, my jo.' I showed it to you in the dictionary last week. Let's see—that's three times eight is twenty-four, plus another twenty-four, plus two for the 'O's is fifty."

"Is it in the dictionary?" Ella asked, using the question as a pretense to thumb through the ragged blue Webster's Collegiate in search of a word for herself.

"You can hear everything I say," Uncle Sol said. "Quit prospecting in there."

"Why can't you leave her alone?" Pete said. He looked toward the doorway, where we were standing. "Evelyn, maybe you can help me with these two babies," he said.

"Oh, it's you," Uncle Sol said, turning around. "See anything you like around the place, girlie? Take what you want, like everyone else."

"It's so beautiful here," Elizabeth said.

"Not like it used to was," Uncle Sol said. "I just can't keep up with the gardens anymore."

"I'll weed for you tomorrow morning, if you like," Elizabeth said sweetly.

"You city girls always pull out the flowers and leave the weeds."

"I'm no city girl, and I know what I'm doing in a garden."

Oh, how he hooks them and reels them in, I thought.

"Whose turn is it?" Ella asked.

"It's yours and you know it," said Uncle Sol. "She's stalling for time, as usual. Come on, you two, I'll show you some skeletons in the closet while this one ponders."

We followed him into the front hall and up the stairs. Elizabeth trailed behind, peeking into the two bedrooms at the top of the stairs. Uncle Sol went back. "I'd forgotten you haven't been here before," he said. "I feel like I've known you all my life—you should be so lucky. You can sleep here." We were in the gray room, above Uncle Sol's bedroom. It has a view of the hills to the east, above which a full moon was now hovering, as if conjured up by Uncle Sol himself.

"What a privilege," I said. "Usually this room is reserved for dignitaries."

"It's for her that I'm letting you stay here, bub."

"You two—I declare," Elizabeth said. "Where are the skeletons?"

Back we went across the hall, then through the yellow room and up the steep steps to the attic. Uncle Sol turned on the light. A big television antenna lay on its side at the far end of the long, peak-roofed room. Along one side stood a row of nine shadowy milk cans. Tall cartons overflowing with books and shoes and cushions and clothes were scattered on the floor. Near us was a small enclave of beautiful old china washbasins and matching pitchers.

"I found them when I was poking around up here the other day," Uncle Sol said. "Why don't you take a couple for your apartment?"

"They're just lovely," Elizabeth said, bending down for a closer look. "But we couldn't just take them. I mean, don't you want to keep them? They must be valuable."

"All this foolishness about antiques," Uncle Sol said. "It's just a lot of nonsense. Anyway, they're of no use to me. Take them. Take anything."

"No—we couldn't," Elizabeth said with finality as she stood up.

"There's a glint in your eye."

"Well, maybe this one." Elizabeth picked up a set that was white with painted blue wildflowers sprinkled over the basin and pitcher.

"Of course she picks the nicest one," Uncle Sol said.

"Oh, for heaven's sake," Elizabeth said, putting the set back down.

"Don't pay any attention to him," I said. "He offered it, take it." She turned to go downstairs. I took her arm and pulled her back gently. "Come on," I said. "He really does want us to have it—I can tell."

"Well, thank you," Elizabeth said to Uncle Sol. "I'm sorry I lost my temper. I guess I'm just not used to that kind of joking."

In bed that night in the executive suite, Elizabeth and I lay propped against the pillows, looking out at the Berkshires, which receded into the distance like gray swells in a motionless gray sea. Uncle Sol was rustling newspapers and knocking around in his room below, and I half expected to hear "Adieu, adieu, adieu. Remember me" float up through the floorboards. Instead, from another quarter came three faint, lonely whistlings from Ella's hearing aid—*oooeee, oooeee, oooeee*—as if somewhere in the back of the house a bos'n were piping an admiral aboard. We got all the way under the covers and drifted toward sleep. Elizabeth whispered that maybe one interesting family was enough. "He hates me, I'm sure," she said, and I wondered whether love was nothing more than a commitment to eternal reassurance. Elizabeth was breathing evenly through her mouth. I began a dream about fencing; I wounded my opponent and then bandaged him (or her?— I couldn't tell through the mask). Elizabeth murmured something about "taking advantage" or "making an advance," but maybe I dreamed that, too.

The morning was clear and cool. The earth and sky glistened with a green-and-blue freshness that made the inside of the house, with its frail cargo of recumbent elders, seem dreary and depressing. Dust was visible everywhere. In the bathroom sink there were rust stains like old dry blood. Near one corner of the Mexican rug in our room was a large bird-shaped hole.

"This place needs work," Elizabeth whispered as we tiptoed around. She picked up the pitcher and washbasin that I now began to think she'd had no intention of not taking; I picked up our suitcases; and we crept downstairs like thieves. When we put the set in the car, we saw Ella just disappearing at the end of the driveway for her constitutional—a two-mile walk that she had been taking every morning, rain or shine, of every summer that I could remember. She carried a cane, as usual—not for support but so that she could swipe at any car that passed too close as she strolled down the middle of the right lane of the narrow road.

In the kitchen, Elizabeth and I assembled a quick, meagre breakfast for ourselves. A thin coat of grease covered everything, and Elizabeth washed the plates and glasses before we used them as well as after. I wanted to get going, but of course we had to wait for Ella to come back and for Pete and Uncle Sol to get up, so that we could say a courteous goodbye. Elizabeth said she would work in the flower beds for a while, and I went out to stow our luggage in the car and put the bike up on the rack. Then I changed Uncle Sol's flat.

Half an hour later Ella sailed back up the driveway, waved her cane at Elizabeth among the lilies, and disappeared inside the house. In fifteen minutes she came out again, sat down in a rocking chair on the porch, and beckoned us over. We sat down on the railing. Ella had oatmeal on her forehead.

"What's up?" I said to her loudly.

"Nothing," she said. "What should be up? I just wanted to look at your pretty faces."

"How was your walk?" said Elizabeth, who would be incapable of raising her voice to shout for help if she were drowning.

Ella smiled as sweetly and vacantly as an infant.

"Jeez, I'd like to get out of here," I said under my breath.

"What's your hurry, mister?" Ella asked. "Is there a fire?"

"You incredible old phony," I said.

She shrugged and grinned.

Just then, Uncle Sol materialized in the kitchen, his face a blur behind the window screens. "If Queen Elizabeth will drive me into town, I'll let her buy me a *Times*," he said.

"I'll go, too," I said.
"No, we're eloping," he said.

I'll never know what Uncle Sol and Elizabeth said to each other on that trip. Elizabeth just doesn't recall the details of conversations. They seem to light up the neurons in her brain and then fade away quickly and entirely, like subatomic particles in a cloud chamber. Maybe that's healthier than hanging on to words like an old miser with his hoard, which is what I do. I don't know. Anyway, as we drove away from the farmhouse that morning all Elizabeth could tell me was "He just asked a lot of questions." What kind of questions? "Oh, I don't know—whether we were going to get married and settle down." And what did you say? "I honestly can't remember." Try. "I said I thought so. No, I hoped so. I don't know what I said." What else? "Nothing, really." Nothing for half an hour? "Oh, I think he was worrying about your politics." What did you say? "Something about your being honest and decent. About your generosity." Thank you. "At least that's what I was thinking. I don't remember whether I actually said it. He may not have even asked me about it. It was just on my mind." What else? "Good heavens, what difference does it make?" *What else?* "He talked about the house." And? "What a burden it was. Or whether I thought you could handle it." There's a big difference. What did you say? "I was thinking how lovely it could be." But what did you *say?* "I don't know."

If this kind of thing didn't happen all the time, I'd have suspected her of artfulness. Of course, it could be that she's artful all the time, though I doubt it. But I don't know for sure. None of us knows anything with any certainty about anyone but himself, and of course even then it's not always clear. Sometimes, late at night, we can tap on the walls, just to tell our neighbors that they aren't alone, but that's about it.

What I do know is this: When Elizabeth and Uncle Sol left

for town, I went out to the brook and sailed leaves down it, the way I did when I was a kid. I looked around. I had a strange premonition that I'd never come here again. I imagined little Socialists running all over the place. It would be a relief—the long-delayed end of my childhood. I lay down and gazed up at the perfect blue sky, and an ant crawled into my ear. They came back. Slam, slam went the car doors, like the reports of distant cannons.

On the porch, Ella, Pete, and Elizabeth sat in a row. "He wants to see you," Elizabeth said. "He's in his room."

"After that we can go," I said.

Through the dining room, through the living room, into Uncle Sol's dim precinct, where the shades are always drawn. Uncle Sol lying on his bed in the far corner, as if marooned on a tiny island. Three digital clocks—presents from three of his August courtiers—on the night table beside his bed, all glowing, one saying 9:15, one saying 10:05, one saying 4:52. The *World* stacked up at the foot. Heavy, dark furniture lowering out of the shadows.

"Sit down here, boy," Uncle Sol said, sweeping a newspaper from the chair beside his bed.

"Aren't you going to have some breakfast, Uncle Sol?"

"I don't feel so hot. My neck hurts like the devil in the morning. And I'm so damned tired all the time. That never used to happen."

"You put in the vegetable garden by yourself."

"That's what you think," he said. "I used some of your last . . . contribution to hire that boy What's-His-Name from Mill River to help me. I'm not complaining, mind you. There's enough wrong in the world. Did you see the front page today? It's a terrible situation all around. It's going to explode at any moment."

"Things do seem pretty bad," I said.

"That's some gal you've got there." He waved toward the porch.

"It's a question of who's got whom."

"She has a fine sense of values, very socially conscious, though she pretends not to be. And she's modest, too—not like some people I know."

"Yeah, she's just great. Well, so I guess we should be going."

"Not so fast, bub. I've got something for you." He held up a key in front of me. It caught a stray ray of light from the door and gleamed like a magic amulet. "It's the key to my safe-deposit box in town. In case something happens to me, which it won't, so don't get your hopes up. I'm going to call the lawyer in town tomorrow—John Whosis—and make an appointment. I've been giving this whole business a lot of thought, and I've found that I can't really think about this place without you being around. You ought to settle down, boy. It's no fun being alone—believe me, I know. Do you think you could take care of the place?"

"Well—"

"Would you come here, at least in the summers?"

"Sure, I—I don't really know what to say."

"You at a loss for words? It's almost worth it."

"I never expected this."

"You've thought about it, haven't you? Tell the truth."

"I guess so."

"Don't think I'm doing this for your father."

"Don't worry."

"I'm doing it for you, and for myself. Don't ask me why. I don't know."

On my way out, I nearly knocked Ella down in the living room.

"The lord of the manor," she said. "Will you have room for an old deaf lady?"

"No," I said, "but I'll have room for you."

It's cooler up here in Vermont than it is in Massachusetts. Elizabeth and I are sitting on the deck, shivering a little and watching the sunset across the lake our cottage fronts on. When you put the lake's water in a glass, there's a disturbing yellow tinge to it, and things nip at you when you go swimming. Elizabeth says, "If we have children, Uncle Sol's will be a wonderful place to raise them."

I'm trying to imagine myself as part of the landed gentry and am having a hard time. I'm also thinking of how I'm going to call my father and give him the news, and about how Uncle Sol made his mind up and then dragged his heels about telling me. Typical.

The Old Left

UNCLE SOL IS SUPPOSED to leave for Mexico next Sunday, escorted by the Blooms, a couple of retired-schoolteacher friends who are younger than he is but still of the Very Old Left. They own a house in San Miguel. They have been in my uncle's thrall ever since they did volunteer work for the settlement house he ran in Brooklyn until he retired, fifteen years ago. But today, which is *this* Sunday, Uncle Sol is having his doubts. He's deep into his eighties now, which is old, no getting around it. He still puts in some unpaid time writing captions for the *Daily World*, and he still calls me "boy," but he doesn't make any more jokes about being middle-aged, and he has stopped saying things like "I'd like to visit Russia again when I grow up." All his doctors have been warning him that to stay in the Northeast for the rest of January and February and March would be dangerous for him. There are a lot of them—a heart specialist for his heart failure, a joint man for the arthritis in his neck and back, an ear-nose-and-throat man for his chronically inflamed sinuses, and an eye man for his aged, tearless eyes. And there are a lot of other people who from a safe distance (usually over the telephone) give advice to Uncle Sol—a few old pals in the city from the Spanish Civil War, ancient Progressives and their children and grandchildren, and locals and summer people up in the Berkshires, where Uncle Sol lives from May through September in his big, red farmhouse. Everyone has been urging him to get out for the winter.

Still, when he called me earlier this morning, an hour or so ago, to maneuver me into offering him a ride to the dentist tomorrow, to have a bad tooth looked at, he seemed to be taking a strange pleasure in describing the swelling of his face and the pain he'd been suffering for the last couple of days. The affliction sounded like an unexpected but welcome guest whom Uncle Sol would have to entertain for some time. "I don't know, Davey," he said feebly on the phone. "If this keeps up, I'll have wings of my own by the end of the week. I won't need to take a plane anywhere."

He didn't ask me to drive him to the dentist. (He never asks me directly to do any of the small favors I do for him when he's in the city, like picking up a prescription for him on a nasty day, helping him balance his checkbook, or spending a couple of hours at his place on a Saturday afternoon while he inveighs against the evils of our system and the lies of the press—this last he pokes at me like a prospector looking for pay dirt, since I was once a reporter at City Hall for the *Times* and now teach at Columbia Journalism School.) He simply asked me to remind him which number bus would take him from Chelsea, where he has an apartment in a city housing project, to Central Park West, where his dentist's office is. When I first said I'd take him, he said, "Don't be ridiculous." But I kept at it until, finally, he found the generousness of spirit to accommodate my stubborn and foolish insistence.

When I hung up, I found my wife, Elizabeth—not Liz, mind you, or Lizzie or Betsy or Beth, but Elizabeth—standing behind me. She has got to know what's going on.

"Why can't he get someone who lives nearer to help?" Elizabeth said. She walked back into the bedroom, where she collapsed on the bed. "I guess nobody else has a car."

"Oh, it's O.K.," I said. "I've got a whole week of semester break left with no papers to grade."

"But you were going to start on course plans for the fall tomorrow," Elizabeth said. She shivered and pulled her bathrobe around her. It turned lethally cold in New York New Year's Day—the worst cold of the century, the papers and television have been calling it, as if it were a circus attraction—and only the bedroom in our apartment has been halfway habitable, because the living room, study, and kitchen all face the Hudson River and the keen, cold winds that rush across it and detonate on Morningside Heights.

"All that can wait," I said. "Listen, if he doesn't get away now, I'm going to have to be running down to his place for the next two or three months. Besides, the Blooms think he's the cat's pajamas, and they have a separate little suite for him down there, and a doctor lives next door. And it's warm. I'd rather take him to the dentist than—"

"The cat's pajamas?" Elizabeth said.

Elizabeth is six years younger than I am—thirty-four. We got married two years ago, when I was thirty-eight. Late. She had come to New York to be assistant curator of the Museum of Natural History's Hall of Marsupials after working at the Endicott Museum in Boston for four years, and after six years of a bad marriage to a fellow biology graduate student, who to this day is working on his thesis at Boston University. Actually, the last I heard, he hadn't even finished the outline. Elizabeth introduced herself to me at the museum, in front of a sort of variety-pack diorama of extinct pouched creatures, and got me to take her out to lunch. Elizabeth's mother and father, who still live in Sharon, Connecticut, where she was born, are in their mid-fifties. *My* parents are in their mid-seventies, having had me in their mid-thirties. Late again, especially for that day and age. Soon I'll have to be running up to Palisades to attend to them, just as I go downtown now for Uncle Sol. And when that sadness is over, Elizabeth's parents will need looking after. And then it will be my turn. And then Elizabeth's. Before all that happens, we want to have a child or two, to balance the future with a little youth and hope.

Anyway, I have a repertoire of antique expressions, like "spooning" and "bub" and "the cat's pajamas" that I learned from Uncle Sol and my parents, and that Elizabeth finds quite hilarious. When I use one of them, or idly sing some vintage popular tune, like "The Band Played On," or "Sleepy Time Gal," Elizabeth raises her eyebrows and looks at me as though one of her fossils had suddenly come to life and turned up in her apartment. It's all very funny, but often at those moments I get the feeling that Elizabeth doesn't really know me and never will— the kind of feeling that until she came along and put me in her pocket had been strong enough to give me a secret excuse for not settling down with anyone. You don't stay unmarried until you're nearly forty unless you think you've got secrets.

It's Sunday night, and Elizabeth and I are eating dinner in front of the television set in the bedroom, wishing we could join the little English girl who with her family is trying to make a go of it in Kenya. It looks very warm in Kenya. The temperature in New York today never got above ten, and now it's five, and the windows in all the other rooms are covered with ice, especially the kitchen, where the water that boiled off while I made spaghetti, under Elizabeth's watchful eye, reappeared quickly as rime on the frigid glass. While the spaghetti was cooking, I went into the living room and with a table knife scraped out a peephole on one of the windows there. On the river, five freighters had dropped anchor during the day; we assumed it was because the ice farther north was impassable. When I peered out, the freighters all had their deck lights on, and they looked like a line of stores in a shopping mall. It must be frustrating for the men on board, who most likely became sailors because they wanted to stay on the move, to sit paralyzed in the middle of what they probably thought was nowhere. Each ship was surrounded by a flange of ice, like a ballerina's tutu, and just before sunset they all pivoted in a cumbersome half pirouette as the tide turned.

Now the little girl is going to get an old Dutch trekker to help her family and their neighbors kill a leopard that has been skulking around their homesteads. "I think it's rather important," she says to the grizzled hunter as she gives him the note from her father. She is handling him as if he were the child and she the adult.

The phone rings in the hall. I go out and answer it and reclose the door, to keep the warmth in.

"Well, where are you, boy?" Uncle Sol says, in a weak voice.

"I'm here at home—what do you mean?" I say.

"Well, it's nine-thirty. Aren't you supposed to pick me up for the dentist now?"

"But that's tomorrow morning, Uncle Sol." The door opens behind me. Elizabeth, *semper vigilis*.

"Is it morning or night?" Uncle Sol asks.

"Night."

"Oh, God, I'm all balled up. I took a sleeping pill. I think I did. But that was at night. It's crazy."

"It's nighttime now, Uncle Sol. You probably took the pill and woke up, and now you're confused."

"Well, this is a fine fettle of kish. O.K., boy, see you tomorrow. If you'd just quit calling me at all hours, maybe I could get some rest."

"Didn't take enough to finish the job, huh?" Elizabeth says after I hang up. "I didn't mean it, I didn't mean it."

"Why aren't you in there keeping an eye on the leopard?" I say.

"I brought you this blanket in case you had to stand out here for a long time," she says.

Uncle Sol and I are waiting for the elevator outside his apartment, on the twenty-first floor. His black overcoat hangs on his small frame like a hand-me-down, and his big bald head looks too heavy for the rest of him. He's wearing his jaunty brown beret. Only artists and Communists wear brown berets. His jaw is badly swollen, I must admit, and he seems weak and still confused, and I can understand a little better how he might fear the prospect of a long trip. He took forever to get ready to leave for the dentist, as I expected he would. In his apartment, he picked up a set of keys, looked at it as though it were a Martian artifact, put it down again, and picked up another. He put on and then took off two pairs of gloves before settling on a third. He gave me a letter he wanted to mail and a little later spent five minutes looking for it, before I figured out what was going on. He's forgetful, of course, but I'd never before seen him so baffled by ordinary tasks. And his place seemed unutterably lonely, with its north view of the tall slabs of Midtown skyscrapers, the desolate West Side, and, farther to the west, the river. It is clear and stunningly cold outside, and far up the river I could make out my five freighters, motionless amid the rubble of ice washing down from somewhere north of the Tappan Zee Bridge, north of my parents' house. And inside, every object—the small upright piano, the television set, the pots and pans in the kitchen, the furniture, the desk top with its windfall of little reminder notes—seemed brushed with the dust of a lonely old age.

The elevator arrives, but instead of getting on, Uncle Sol turns around and walks back to his door.

"Where are you going now?" I say.

"Timbuktoo—where do you think?" he says.

He lets himself in and reappears almost immediately with a small black leather bag.

"You look like you're about to make a house call," I say. "What have you got in there?"

"Wait-and-see pudding," he says.

Finally we get down to the street. Just before we reach the car, a terrific gust of wind comes along and nearly sends Uncle Sol sprawling into a dirty, icy snowbank. I reach out to steady him, and am surprised at the raptorlike strength with which he grasps my arm. "Aren't you ashamed of yourself—pushing an old man," he says, shading his eyes against the sun. I open the door for him, and he eases himself into the front seat as if he were dangerous cargo, I go around to the driver's side, and we're off at last.

Traffic is slow. Pedestrians, bundled up as round as onions, are crossing against the lights because they can't bear to stand still in the raw, blustery weather. For no particular reason that I can see, Uncle Sol starts a story about my mother and father's wedding. We stop at a red light, and I look over at him and see that he is nearly enveloped by the bucket seat. His eyes are far away. I think I know this story—these twelve stories, I should say. "Well, your father did get nervous after all," Uncle Sol says. "He couldn't seem to forget that Emily's father didn't approve of the marriage. I'd gotten to know the old man—we had become good friends—and I can assure you it wasn't because our family was Jewish or radical or anything like that. No, it was because your father was so handsome and charming that he was kinda spoiled, and the old boy wasn't sure how responsible he would be as a husband." I was right. I do know this complicated tale, almost by heart. It used to be that Uncle Sol's stories enchanted me, even after I learned that they involved considerable embroidery. He had a way of making me and himself and the rest of my family seem colorful and funny and sometimes heroic, of endowing our lives with a kind of shape and meaning. That bright gift has become tarnished by the garrulousness of age, and I often find myself daydreaming like this instead of listening. "Oh, Emily was a knockout herself," Uncle Sol says. "But she was bright and serious besides—a most remarkable gal, as she still is. So, as I was saying, your father was so nervous that he took a flask with him when I drove him to the church, and . . ."

My mother's parents will watch in shock as my father takes a swig from a flask while Uncle Sol drives him past the church. Later, Uncle Sol's role as peacemaker will loom larger and larger, until he has become the principal figure in the marriage. It is as if he had married the marriage. The enchantment has given way to a kind of desperate self-reassurance. Maybe it was that all along, only better disguised.

We stop for another light at Fifty-seventh Street. Uncle Sol has come to the end of a chapter, and, in case I think he has finished, he utters a drawn-out "So," as if he were beginning a new verse of the kind of old-time ballad that would cause Elizabeth's eyebrows to rise.

"There's no reason this should keep you from going away," the dentist tells Uncle Sol as we're about to leave his office. "Barring complications, of course," he adds, peering over his eyeglasses for admonitory effect. The catch is that Uncle Sol will have to have three more appointments during the week.

We are standing at the elevator, when Uncle Sol turns to me and says, "Are you in a hurry?" I say no. "Of course you are," he says. "But you're just going to have to hold your horses. I have some private business to attend to. Wait here." He takes from me the little black bag that he had almost forgotten to bring along this morning and totters back down the hall toward the dentist's receptionist. I follow him. He puts the bag down on the receptionist's desk, opens it, and takes out a clear plastic bag containing four or five potatoes. "Something for you from the country," he says to the receptionist, a West Indian woman with an extremely reserved manner. She breaks into a delighted smile, as if she'd just been named Queen of the Bahamas and were being presented with the crown jewels, and thanks Uncle Sol profusely. What is private about this? Is it that he has no potatoes for me? Or did he trick me into following him? When he turns around and sees me standing there, he says, "Well, if it isn't Mr. Nosy Parker."

I returned from Uncle Sol's after four. I did some shopping, went home, and in the face of three more such dental odysseys fell asleep. When Elizabeth came home from work, she woke me from a dream in which I was trying to drive a Galápagos tortoise to Mexico in a truck that wouldn't start moving because vines and tendrils, anchored to huge rocks under the surface of the soil, were growing out of its sides and tires. I got up, and Elizabeth and I huddled together in the kitchen for warmth while I made some salad and some saffron rice and cleaned and sautéed the shrimp I'd bought on the way back from putting the car in the garage. Elizabeth coached me on the rice and the shrimp.

Once again, we are eating in the bedroom. The outdoor-indoor thermometer in the living room says four and fifty-two, and the blanket that Elizabeth hung over the door to the living room is stirring in the draft like a ghost's robe. The freighters are still moored there, in the middle of the river, pointing upstream after another imperceptibly slow tidal sweep.

"Nosy Parker?" Elizabeth says quizzically, after I describe the potato episode for her. "Is that some kind of Australian slang?"

"And on the way back to his place," I go on, like a witness warming to his own testimony, "he took a half an hour to explain to me how he had managed to persuade someone to participate in the sixties antiwar demonstrations."

"It's going to be a rough week," Elizabeth says.

"He told me how he had made this person read the *Daily World* and practically dragged him to the Moratorium marches."

"How extremely annoying that must have been for the person," Elizabeth says.

"The trouble is, this whole conversion story was a complete fabrication, because it was my brother Nick he was talking about."

"Oh, no!"

"He just sat there and bald-facedly said, 'And then, Davey, don't you remember, I made the train reservations for both of us, because I knew Nick would end up doing the right thing.'"

"And did you correct him?"

"I said, 'Look, Uncle Sol, oddly enough I happened to know my own brother fairly well, and I can tell you that he didn't read the *Daily World* and he took a bus to Washington all by himself.'"

"And what did he say?"

"He said, 'I'm surprised at you, boy. I didn't know you had such a bad temper. To say nothing of your memory.'"

"Yes, it's a wonder he can put up with you," Elizabeth says.

Elizabeth was right. It has been a rough week. A rough six days, I should say, since today is Sunday. Uncle Sol takes off for Mexico in a few hours. I mean, he's supposed to. Every day he has told me that he doesn't think he's going to make it, even though the swelling in his jaw has gone way down and he has complained about his pain only when he remembered to. I'm lying here in bed trying to figure out why he's dragging his heels up to the last minute like this, especially since many past winters have seen him depart, with no louder complaint than "I don't really want to go but they're begging me," for a stay with one of his old Progressive friends who long ago gave up New York's ideological and climatic extremes for Arizona, California, and Mexico. The only thing I can come up with is that for the first time in his life, he really believes that he's not too far away from death, and that he wants to die at home. Maybe he thinks of New York as his Kremlin, and that if he dies somewhere outside its walls he will have been caught out in some kind of geographical revisionism.

He has also been warning his escorts for the trip, the patient

Blooms, that he might decide to stay behind. Every night he has called them and every night they have called me, to ask me what I think the chances are. My father has been calling me, too, to ask the same question and to apologize for being too old to be his brother's keeper, and so have some of Uncle Sol's other friends. I've been urging the trip on him—quietly and subtly, I thought, until Friday, after his last dentist appointment. When I dropped him off and promised to go back down this morning and help him pack if he decided to go, he said, with an edge of bitterness, "You can't wait to see the last of me, can you?"

That was merely the most direct evidence that Uncle Sol had put me on trial. During the week I've been told that the CIA is solely responsible for the unrest in Poland, that my interest in food is probably a sign of moral degeneracy, that members of the Moral Majority shouldn't even be allowed to speak, and that it's a crime to let people have private cars in the city—this last just after we'd driven past a subway station with a token line that for some subterranean reason extended up the stairs and halfway down the block.

We were on our way to pick up some Percodan that the dentist had prescribed for Uncle Sol. I'd bet it was that Percodan, in combination with a Seconal, or one of the other narcotics that Uncle Sol has on hand and on occasion dips into at the wrong time of day, that caused Thursday's frightening Unscheduled Appearance. It was the coldest day so far, and the only one that held any promise of being uncle-free. Even the bedroom was cold, and to be able to sit still and read I'd not only put on many layers of clothing but wrapped myself in Elizabeth's voluminous Icelandic-wool shawl. At about four-thirty, having stuffed myself into an armchair and feeling like somebody's granny, I got a call from Uncle Sol's dentist. He said that Uncle Sol had just shown up, looking woozy and pale, for a nonexistent appointment. Had he left again? Yes.

Oh, terrific! Uncle Sol, who shunned taxis as if they were as retrograde as royal litters, was out there somewhere, stunned by drugs, staggering through the frozen twilight to catch a bus that would probably land him in front of a gutted tenement in the South Bronx. Even if he got the right one, he had a tough two-block cross-town walk at the other end against the cutting Arctic winds to get to his place.

Elizabeth got home a little after five, her nose and ears as red as stoplights. When I told her what was going on, she looked utterly stricken. "That poor old man," she said.

"Poor old man my ass," I said. "He's doing it so that he'll get sick and won't be able to leave. He's doing it to make us worry about him. God forbid I should go one day without him at the center of my attention." But in my mind I saw him fighting his way through the deepening gloom of Chelsea, going slower and slower, as if in a dream, and finally freezing in his tracks in the midst of his abstractly beloved poor, his hand up to hold his thin and pitifully rakish brown beret against the wind. I only hoped that his eyes were filled with euphoric visions of a world without taxis or tuxedos, that his ears were ringing with the "Internationale," and his soul was brimming with joy as Marx and Engels, their beards even more magnificent than they had been in life, gathered him from the dark streets and into the bosom of a stateless, profitless, Godless paradise.

Together, Elizabeth and I, fat with clothes, paced the bedroom waiting till it made sense to start calling him at home. Then I dialed him every five minutes for half an hour, and just before I was going to hang up and call in the police to start looking for a petrified Communist with the *World* folded into the pocket of his overcoat, he picked up the phone. He was all right.

I get to Uncle Sol's place at about nine. The limousine that the Blooms have hired to pick him up and then them for the trip out to LaGuardia is due at ten. I knock on Uncle Sol's door and let myself in with the set of keys he gave me a long time ago, "so that the undertaker won't have to break the door down," as he put it. He is sitting in his living room reading the Sunday *Times*, which his neighbor, a Puerto Rican woman he has been trying to indoctrinate for ten years, bought for him on her way back from early Mass. He hasn't done any packing.

"What are you doing here, bub?" he says to me, looking over his glasses. "You were supposed to call first."

"I decided to take matters into my own hands," I say.

"You're just going to ship me off, huh? Well, I'm sorry, Davey, but I think I may not be up to it. I was just about to call the Blooms."

"Where's your suitcase?"

"Listen to him," Uncle Sol says.

"You're going; I've decided for you," I say. I find a large leather suitcase in a closet off the hall between the living room and the bedroom. I take it into the bedroom and open it on the bed, which is made, and neat as a pin. "I'm starting with your delicate underthings," I call to Uncle Sol. "If there's anything you think you're going to have particular need of in Siberia, you better let me know."

I hear Uncle Sol shuffling in the hall. He stands in the doorway to his bedroom and watches me as I open one of the drawers in his dresser, a handsome old thing, mahogany, and almost as tall as its proprietor.

"So the Cossacks have finally arrived," Uncle Sol says. "Look on the top of the dresser. I found it in my desk the other day."

I do, and there is a silver-framed picture of me from my college graduation, looking as though I had nothing more to learn.

"Too bad you've regressed so badly since then," Uncle Sol says.

"I'm not the only one," I say, beginning to pack.

"O.K., this has gone far enough," he says.

I straighten up and face him. "Listen, if you can take four hours in no degrees traipsing all over the city and waiting for buses and giving your relatives heart attacks, you can sit on a plane for five hours to Mexico."

"You know what's best for me, do you?" he says.

"That's right."

"You don't."

"Oh, all right, I give up," I say. I start to unpack the few things I've put in the suitcase.

"Don't sulk," Uncle Sol says.

"Well, it's ridiculous."

"Everyone is just trying to get rid of me," Uncle Sol says, with not quite enough irony.

"I'm not," I say, and slam the drawer closed. "I'm trying to keep you."

Uncle Sol scrutinizes me as if he were trying to read some complicated meteorological instrument. "Well, then," he says, "the least you could do is use the right suitcase. It's in the closet behind you."

"Someday you will drive me as crazy as you already are," I say, wheeling around and snatching the other suitcase from the closet.

"When you're finished in here," Uncle Sol says, "you can go into the kitchen and pack the potatoes."

It's Sunday night, and Elizabeth and I are having dinner in front of the TV again, watching the apparently endless series about the masterful little English girl. We turned it on a bit late, and I'm having trouble distinguishing one young frontiersman with a mustache from another. Actually, there is a dark one with a mustache, a blond one with a mustache, and a blond one without a mustache. Elizabeth flattered me into watching the show by telling me that the dark one looked like me. Anyway, the wife of one of these men is having an affair with another of them, probably because she can't tell them apart, either. It's all too much for me, and to keep from eating too fast in the presence of narrative confusion

[68]

and the absence of conversation, I get up and walk out to the living room. It became habitable again this afternoon, with the day's rising temperatures and falling winds. In fact, when I got home from Uncle Sol's at about one, after Uncle Sol was picked up by the Tel Aviv limousine service (which he grumbled about, because of the Zionism implicit in its name), I found Elizabeth in the process of reclaiming the front part of our apartment. Sun was streaming in the living-room windows, and Elizabeth, having dusted and swept and watered all the plants, which seem to have flourished in the chilliness, was playing hymns on the piano.

"Did he get away all right?" she asked.

"Yes—barely," I said.

"What a relief. Well, he's probably over Missouri right now, making them earn their wings."

"I had to convince him that I wasn't just trying to get him out of my hair. I told him it was only because I cared about him. The thing is, I'm not sure it's true."

"Of course it's true," Elizabeth said. She turned back to the piano and started picking out "After the Ball."

"When did you learn that?" I said.

"I heard you humming it when you were making the marinade last night," she said. "It's pretty. What's it called?"

Now I'm standing in the dark at the window. Elizabeth comes and stands beside me. She kisses me on the cheek. "It's nothing but shots of water buffalo right now," she says. "Look—there's another freighter way down at the end of the line. Can you see it?"

"So there is," I say.

"If this thaw keeps up, they'll probably leave soon."

"I hope so," I say. "They're beginning to get on my nerves."

The Ravages of Time

L AST MAY, I CANCELLED my classes for a week, and my wife,
Elizabeth, and I took Uncle Sol up from the public-housing
project in Chelsea where he lives during the winter to his big red
farmhouse in Sheffield, Massachusetts—which, owing to Elizabeth's charm and an otherwise imperceptible doctrinal mellowing
in his old age, Uncle Sol recently decided to bequeath not to the
Alliance of Socialist Youth, or whatever it was, but to me. Dave.
Though I shall be "Davey" to Uncle Sol even if I am knighted
or win the Nobel Prize or am named Emperor of the Universe.
The flexibility of the academic calendar is one of the reasons I quit
my job as a City Hall reporter some years back and went to teach
at Columbia's journalism school. I guess I never quite outgrew
the child's expectation of a couple of weeks off in the winter,
another in the spring, and three months in the summer. Also, I
didn't like the venality of the politics I was covering, so I ac-
cepted the university's invitation and took refuge among its quieter
follies and plenitudinous vacations. And, anyway, as the years at
the newspaper went by I grew to hate writing. One writer is
enough in any family. Elizabeth, who quit her job as a curator at

the Museum of Natural History just before Charlie came along, now writes serious pieces about psychology for serious magazines. She enjoys it.

When we drove down to Chelsea from the three-and-a-half-tiny-bedroom upper-West Side apartment that we moved to after our son, Charles, arrived, we found Uncle Sol outside his place, standing on the sidewalk next to a huge old leather suitcase with twine wrapped around it a few times. The sun was out and it was balmy, but Uncle Sol, hypochondria in full spring bloom, had on a heavy, oversize wool overcoat and the usual brown beret. He is nearly ninety years old—all knobs, strings, bones, and dome—and in this getup he looked like an unshelled tortoise wrapped in a musty tweed curtain.

This would be the first real encounter between Uncle Sol and Charlie, who was ten months old. They had met once before, at the end of the previous summer, up in the country, just after Charlie was born, but the baby was still oblivious of the world around him, and Uncle Sol was almost completely supine, since he was recovering from severe pneumonia that had developed from a cold. The illness had put him in the hospital for a few days, which gave me a little time to batten down the house for the winter. When he was discharged, it seemed that his few remaining traces of geniality and humor had disappeared. I must confess that it was a relief to drive away with Elizabeth and Charlie and his infant paraphernalia, and leave Uncle Sol's transportation down to the city in the hands of a doctor and his wife who had a summer house nearby.

During the fall and winter, I went to visit Uncle Sol at his apartment alone. Elizabeth willingly stayed at home with Charlie and the chores that sprang up around him like weeds. I would have stayed away, too, but I had no choice in the matter. Not only was Uncle Sol one of the very few remnants of my family's older generation, but as a boy I had spent my summers at his house, so my inheritance of it would be a kind of physical com-

plement of an already rich, intangible legacy: however impa-
tiently, he had taught me how to use a rifle, play the guitar, ride
a horse, bid at an auction, paint a barn, row a boat, drive a car,
play poker, and regard wealth with suspicion. To have aban-
doned him to the housekeeper I hired for him and Meals on Wheels
and the kindness of his housing-project neighbors would have
been abandoning part of myself. For some reason, after the pneumonia he seemed able to summon up only bad memories—squa-
lor and fear in the trenches in the First World War, rejection by
women he claimed he had wanted to marry, a schism with my
father over politics, government harassment during the thirties
and forties—and he needed someone to tell them to. So on one
or two afternoons a week I would go to him and, on a glacially
slow trip through the snow to the drugstore or poring over the
jumble of his financial affairs, I would listen. Sometimes, as the
windows in his overheated apartment fogged over, he would begin talking about an attack of diarrhea or vomiting he had suf-
fered recently, and I admit that the only way I could go on sitting
there was to think about my wife and son, contented at home as
the evening came on.

The big question in my mind on the way to Uncle Sol's in
May was how would Uncle Sol, who had been around almost a
hundred times longer than Charlie and had become so difficult to
please, get along with him. It started off well. After refusing Elizabeth's offer of the front, Uncle Sol clambered and creaked into
the back, wagging his cane around this way and that, and finally
came to rest alongside Charlie's car seat. He went to put the cane
on the floor, but Charlie managed to grab the curved end during
one of its passes.

"So this is What's-His-Name," Uncle Sol said. He tried to
reclaim his cane, but Charlie held on tight. "You won't need one
of these things for a while yet," Uncle Sol said, whereupon Charlie unleashed one of his Devastator smiles, which he seldom does

for anyone but us, and yanked the cane entirely free of his grand-uncle's feeble grip.

"I bet you two think he's pretty cute," Uncle Sol said.

"He'll do," I said as I started the car.

"He doesn't smile like that at everyone," Elizabeth said.

"She's exactly like you," Uncle Sol said to Charlie. "Both trying to get on my good side."

"Good luck to them in that case," I said.

We pulled away from Uncle Sol's building and the rest of the gigantic project, in which teemed a portion of the proletarian masses whom Uncle Sol, at least theoretically, champions.

"Who brought the suitcase down on the elevator for you?" I asked into the rearview mirror, knowing where the question would lead.

"Whattayacaller's son Whosis from down the hall," Uncle Sol said. That, as I expected, would be Felix Rodriguez, the baleful teen-ager who lives with his mother next door to Uncle Sol, and to whom I had slipped fifty bucks last November, to run errands for the old man. Uncle Sol had been propagandizing Mrs. Rodriguez for a few years; with long, confusing explanations, he urged her to vote for Gus Hall for President, and he pointed out to her how wonderful it was that that blind black guy, Something or Other Winston, was Party Chairman. "That boy is developing an excellent set of values," Uncle Sol said. What the Rodriguezes made of Uncle Sol and his vague but relentless ideology I could not even begin to guess; I just hoped that they could see at least something of the man he once had been in the man he was. "I was pretty much under the weather for the whole winter, as you know," he went on, "and that boy would do anything I'd ask him to at the drop of a hat and didn't expect a cent in return."

We stopped in traffic on Eleventh Avenue in the Thirties, the construction site of that gargantuan boondoggle the new convention center. Surrounding us, paralyzed by some union squabble, were mammoth yellow earthmovers and cranes, and in their long shadows strolled hard-looking ladies whose shoe heels were longer than their skirts. How remote, there and then, seemed an old man's utopian dreams. "Now, really, Sol, what do you think of Charles?" Elizabeth said. There was no reply from the back seat, and Elizabeth turned around. "Take a look, Dave," she said. I turned, too, to see Charlie asleep with his chin on his chest and one small hand still holding the cane, and Uncle Sol with his eyes closed and his head back, as if he were trying to remember something from a long, long time ago.

The stream that winds down from the Berkshire Hills behind Uncle Sol's house had overflowed the rough plank bridge that marked the boundary between the farthest reach of lawn in front of the house and what used to be a cow pasture, just above the orchard. Cows have not grazed there for nearly twenty years— ever since John Powers died. Mr. Powers was a dairy farmer who lived down the road. There was an extraordinarily fruitful crab-apple tree at his place, and every September Uncle Sol would round up some of his young admirers and me and my brother Nick and go down to Mr. Powers' and send a few guys up into the tree to shake it while the rest of us stood underneath holding blankets to catch the results. In return for that, and for milk and cream and so on, Uncle Sol let Mr. Powers pasture his cows in the meadows around his place. To get hit on the head by those crab apples was nothing more than fun, even for a little boy, and they pelted down in what seemed to me miraculous abundance, like something in the Bible. No less miraculous was the way Uncle Sol, complaining about the work and ordering me and Nick around the kitchen, transformed the sour noggins into sweet jelly, which he would give away to his visitors, who came up from the city in even greater numbers at the end of the summer than at the start or in the middle. As the leaves outside began their colorful demise, the people at Uncle Sol's would dance to his square-dance calling, listen to his stories, sing songs with him, and tolerate his condemnation, good-humored back then, of their profligate materialism. When the last of them left, Uncle Sol and Nick and I closed the house and went back to the city ourselves, he to his work running a settlement house and we to our Progressive private school in the Village, where our teachers called us "people" and we called them by their first names. Uncle Sol had outlasted almost all his old friends; his visitors had dwindled to a mere trickle, and he had spent most of the last few summers alone, except for some visits from me and Elizabeth and a few others. He hasn't put up jelly or anything else for years.

I was recounting some of this ancient history for Elizabeth as we stood in contemplation of the little rogue creek. We had been at Uncle Sol's for a week, and would be leaving the next day, Sunday. When I got to the part about shaking the tree, I found that I couldn't go on. Unconscious for a moment of the bright, cool May morning washed clean and clear by an apocalyptic thunderstorm the night before, I was suffused with the slanting orange light of the early-autumn afternoons of my boyhood. I saw young Communists silhouetted in branches high above me, the sound of the water became the sound of leaves being rattled, and I half expected crab apples to rain down upon us. I was, in a word, mush—maybe in part because our visit, however vexed, was almost over—and to hide it I turned around and picked up Charlie, who was sitting on the lawn behind us, having another and still very uncertain encounter with grass. Every time we put him down on it during the week, he had avoided touching it; he held his hands out over it as if he were afraid it would grow rapidly and need to be held in check. Charlie didn't notice the ridiculous tears that had welled up in his late-early-middle-aged father's eyes. He was just happy to be lifted away from something he felt ought to be wood or concrete or at least fake Oriental but wasn't.

"You're sad," Elizabeth said.

"I was just trying to remember something."

"We should have dug this silt out to get the water down," Elizabeth said. "The boards are going to rot."

Charlie gestured like a maestro toward the creek and shouted, "Dada!" This is what he called almost everything that interested him—trees, garbage trucks, Elizabeth, and the entire Columbia University campus. The rest of his working vocabulary was "kitty" and "booey." The last he applied exclusively to me and to food.

"We should have done a lot of things," I said, "but with Uncle Sol around it would be hard to start the real work that has to be done on this place, even if he let us. It would be like building his coffin while he looked on."

Charlie started squirming with boredom in my arms, so we headed back toward the house. When we got there, I set Charlie down, to let him go *mano a mano* with the lawn once more. He started to crawl nowhere in particular, then he got scared of the botany all over again, reassumed his wary, hands-out position, and raised his eyes to the red pile before him. This is what he saw: peeling paint, dry rot under the eaves which had eaten out a doorway for squirrels, clotted, flaking white gutters with downspouts akimbo, screens with a lot of rips and fewer patches, a sagging porch, cracked windowpanes, a leaky slate roof, a woodshed whose sliding doors didn't, flower beds giving way at their borders to grass choked with ajuga and dandelions. What he didn't see, inside, was a haywire, jerry-built electrical system, mice in the cupboards, a sweating freezer in the cellar filled with dubious food, an ancient, whistling furnace with a loose fan belt, nails poking up from the floors in the second-story bedrooms, six flashlights that didn't work, plumbing of capillary straitness, and a collection of photographs, crockery, shoes, chairs, clocks, pots, blankets, toys, sheet music, tools, racquets, records, radios, letters, footstools, luggage, scarves, books, pipes, and cushions that had started accumulating fifty years ago, when Uncle Sol bought the place, and hadn't stopped since. I held my hand out and said, toward the little blond head below, "Someday all this will be yours." A large woodchuck peered out from under the porch and then made a fat dash across the lawn.

"Kitty!" Charlie shouted.

"Try some of this," Uncle Sol had said to me the night before, while I was cooking dinner. He waggled a fork with some kind of black-green matter on it in front of my face. The day had been gray and humid for May, and now thunder was rumbling around somewhere in the hills across the valley from Uncle Sol's.

"What is it?" I asked.

"Pickled tomatoes. You never tasted anything so good."

"No, thanks," I said, with an emphatic stroke of the cleaver to the second joint of a chicken leg.

"You used to love my pickles," Uncle Sol said.

"I just don't want any."

"You just don't want any."

"That's right."

"I opened this especially for you," Uncle Sol said. He slammed the jar down on the counter where I was working.

"They look spoiled," I said, extracting the giblets in their neat wrapping from inside the chicken carcass.

"Just like yourself," Uncle Sol said. "And that son of yours, if you keep on with him the way you're going. Come on now, boy, I'm telling you to take a bite." From upstairs, far away in the front bedroom, where we had set up Charlie's crib—an industrial-green relic from Uncle Sol's attic that I had slept in when I was a baby—came an attenuated wail of bedtime protest, like a ribbon of aroma in a cartoon.

"No, thanks, really," I said.

"Why do you always say no to what I offer you?"

"Listen, Sol, I'm sorry, but the food you have around here is just too old. A lot of things from the freezer have been thawed and refrozen, and you open things and don't refrigerate them."

"And you'd rather let perfectly good stuff go to waste and drive into town and spend money, even with the world in the state it's in."

"I just like to be careful," I said.

"Enough of this nonsense, Davey. These pickles are excellent, and you're going to try them." Another vaporous cry, this one tinged with resignation, drifted down from the bedroom.

"Oh, all right," I said, and nibbled from the fork that Uncle Sol was once again waving in front of my face.

"What did I tell you?" Uncle Sol said.

"They don't seem right to me," I said. "Let me see the jar." I picked it up and read the label: "Pickled tomatoes, 11/73," it said. "Christ, Sol, this is eleven years old."

"It is not."

"What do you mean? That's what the label says."

"They're almost brand-new."

"Then why does it say eleven seventy-three?"

"I was just using some old labels the other day—last fall," Uncle Sol said. He ostentatiously took a large mouthful of the kelp-like mess. "I don't like being called a liar," he said. He shuffled over to the sink, threw the fork into it, and held his head, as if in the grip of a sudden migraine. "I'm beginning to wonder if our relationship is what I thought it was."

Elizabeth appeared in the kitchen doorway, to the accompaniment of a remote peal of thunder. Uncle Sol was staring out the window, searching for something—anything—that might bear witness to the disrespect he was suffering at my hands. I turned my back to him and loaded the chicken into the oven.

"He's asleep," Elizabeth said. I turned around again, and she held up an empty formula bottle in triumph. "So, let's eat."

"I just started this," I said, "so you'll simply have to wait another forty-five minutes."

Elizabeth looked at me and then at Uncle Sol, and then said, "Oh, no, not again."

What she meant was that after the smooth sailing on the trip up from the city the week's anchorage at Uncle Sol's had been filled with almost nothing but muttering, discontent, and hostility on the part both of the superannuated captain and of his crew. On Sunday, Elizabeth and I—together, during Charlie's long naps, and alone, when he was awake—took down the storm windows and put up the screens. "Wait a minute," said Uncle Sol, hovering over or under us and gesturing with his cane at each new step in the procedure. Wait a minute and wash the ponderous windows, even though so much of the glass was broken; wait a minute and brush the screens, even though they were falling apart; wait a minute, the windows have never been stacked there before—they go over here, all of two feet away, and have to be restacked.

On Monday, Elizabeth tried putting in some begonias under the mock-orange bush near the horse barn. Uncle Sol, emerging onto the porch from the trapdoor to the cellar, where he had been poking around in the freezer for some detritus to serve at supper, thanked her for her efforts but said that the plants were the wrong thing to plant, the place was the wrong place, and the time was the wrong time.

ELIZABETH: I was just trying to help.

SOL: I'm sure you were, Miss, but it's no help at all if it isn't done right.

ELIZABETH (*throwing down her trowel*): I give up.

SOL: Don't forget to put that whattayacallit back where it belongs.

On Tuesday, Uncle Sol and I had a confrontation over mowing the lawn. He said I was doing it in the wrong *pattern*—that it would be harder to rake if it wasn't done up the middle first and then etc., etc. Since it was me who would be doing the raking, I argued a little, and he retired to his bed with what he described as an attack of "needles" in his neck and back.

On Wednesday, it rained, and we sat in the living room after

breakfast and argued about the Russian intervention in Afghani-
stan. This provoked a session of inheritance torture that consisted
of Uncle Sol airily musing about the possibility of giving fifty of
his sixty acres to the Communist Party for a "progressive" children's camp. And, speaking of children, it was Uncle Sol's constant refrain during the week, when he wasn't saying wait a minute
to our maintenance and horticultural efforts, that we were trying
to spoil Charlie. If he dropped a toy and we picked it up for him,
we were overindulging him. If we allowed him to beg a bite of
a cookie from us, we were letting him get away with murder.
This in spite of Charlie's generally excellent behavior, and in
spite of the burgeoning friendship between the two of them.
Uncle Sol played with Charlie for half hours on end—tugging
on the cane, banging the piano in the dining room, playing
which-hand-is-it-in when Charlie crawled up to him on the porch
and gave him a dandelion blossom. At one point Uncle Sol donned
a tall, conical orange party hat, an artifact lying around among
the clutter, dating no doubt from the Halloween of 1938 or 1939,
and Charlie was transported by mirth. That was after dinner
on Wednesday, and Charlie got so worked up that it took
him an extra hour to go to sleep. His crying brought renewed
charges from Uncle Sol in the kitchen while I was washing the
dishes. He somehow managed to link my poor performance as
a father to my retrograde geopolitics, and, for good measure, told
me that seeing how much hot water I used had given him a gassy
stomach.

It was sad to be around someone who had almost completely
outlived his own personality, especially since I had no choice
about continuing to love him. It was also unbearable for a solid
week, so on Thursday Elizabeth and Charlie and I got in our car
and took off for the day. At about seven-thirty that evening, ten
miles from Uncle Sol's, Charlie's patience with the car seat, which
we had lifted him in and out of six or seven times—when we
stopped for tag sales and sightseeing and wholesome junk food

—gave out entirely, so we pulled off the road near a little cemetery at the foot of a mountain and let him play there for a while. The grass was short and unintimidating, and there were big rugs of moss here and there. Charlie, now in the one-piece bright-red pajamas that we had put on him in the hope that he would go to sleep in the car, crawled and chuckled above the dead, hiding from us, tracing chiselled inscriptions with his baby-carrot fingers, and pausing every now and then to point and shout "Dada!" at nothing, or everything. At the back of the cemetery there was a family plot that lay in the last of the day's sunlight. Charlie made his way over to it, emerging from the evening shadows into the sun like a flame. What celestial tree was this lovely child shaken down from, I wondered, and how were we lucky enough to catch him? He pushed himself up against one old gravestone and, taking a lurching half step, extended his hand to touch its twin, which stood a few inches away. He rocked from one foot to the other and did some deep knee bends. If Charlie's little hornpipe disturbed their rest, neither Martha Wheaton, b. 1784 d. 1860 aet. 76, mother of Virginia, Frederick, Mary, Emily, and William, nor her husband, John, let on.

On Friday, I arranged through the local Area Council on Aging for a homemaker to come to Uncle Sol's place three afternoons a week. Before I started the seven phone calls and the two trips to Great Barrington which the job ended up requiring, I told Uncle Sol what I was going to do. He bitterly opposed the idea and would not sign the necessary forms until I confirmed the obvious—yes, he could send away whoever turned up—and, torturing logic, made the case that I had already made in the city under similar circumstances the previous fall: that he would be helping the cause of Socialism if he availed himself of free government services.

Friday evening was the pickles.

Friday night, in our saggy bed, I lay awake, waiting for the first pang of botulism. In his saggy crib in the room next door, Charlie lay sleeping. A thunderstorm was still knocking around the countryside. I thought Elizabeth was asleep, too—like Charlie, she sleeps long and soundly; I'm the one who usually mans the tower at night—but then she turned toward me and said, "I promise you they have too much acid and salt to go really bad."

"That's not what I was thinking about," I said.

"What, then?"

"I was thinking about . . . about, um, the ravages of time."

"You mean what eleven years might do to a jar of pickled tomatoes?"

"I swear that wasn't on my mind at all. I was just thinking about Uncle Sol having grown old and cranky, about me being fifty-something when Charlie is ten—I won't even be able to show him how to run a buttonhook, for Christ's sake."

"Just as well, if that's something in football," Elizabeth said.

"And the house. We'll get it, we'll fix it up a little, we'll leave it to Charlie—and then he'll let it go, and then two hundred years from now it will fall down, and in five hundred years the whole thing will be a field or woods. Or some kind of futuristic mall."

"Those aren't all exactly ravages," Elizabeth said, stifling a yawn.

"And Charlie—he's going to get old and thaw and refreeze food, too, you know."

"We won't be around to see it, though."

"That's a big help."

"I know why you have trouble sleeping, if that's the kind of thing going through your head."

"Well, you asked."

"The way I see it is if all there is is the ravages of time, then you might as well enjoy them," Elizabeth said. She put her arm around my shoulders. "As in fact you do," she added.

I drifted off, I guess. The next thing I knew, we were both sitting bolt upright, with brilliant lights flashing into our room and

[8 2]

huge detonations sounding all around us and water cascading down on the roof. The cold phosphorescence on the hands of the evil-looking little Moskva clock that Uncle Sol had given me when he came back from visiting Russia many years before indicated that it was three-thirty. Elizabeth said, "If you're here, where's Mom?," and I said, "In the lucky hotel," and then we both woke up and realized that a storm had moved right on top of us, and a few seconds later we separated out from its amazing din Charlie's loud crying from next door. We leapt out of bed and went into his room. Lightning gave us erratic glimpses of Charlie standing up in the crib, wide-eyed with fear, shrieking his head off. Elizabeth turned on a lamp, and I picked him up. His body was rigid with terror, and he pushed away from me. Elizabeth took him, but he stiff-armed her, too, and kept on crying. We futilely traded him back and forth, until on the fifth or sixth exchange, with the storm outside already abating, Charlie, who was still going strong, looked over my shoulder and stopped crying as suddenly as if someone had flipped a switch. I turned and saw Uncle Sol, leaning on his cane, in long johns gray with age, and with his wizard-like orange Halloween hat on his head. Charlie pointed toward him and smiled and said, "Dada," tears still oozing out of his eyes.

"What's all the yelling about?" Uncle Sol said. He shuffled over to us and held out a closed hand to Charlie. Charlie pried it open, to discover half a cookie. He said, "Booey," picked up the cookie, took a bite, and yawned enormously.

"Ha, I guess I still know a thing or two," Uncle Sol said. And then, to Charlie, "If you're not careful, you're going to turn out just like your father—always bellyaching."

So when Charlie woke up loud and cheerful the next morning, we decided to carry him out to the stream for a while, to let Uncle Sol have a little extra sleep after his exertions of the night. Taking his absurd hat on and off, feeding Charlie the cookie, he had quieted him until he was nearly asleep in my arms. Then, waving away our whispered thanks as if they were so much smoke in his eyes, and saying how much his legs hurt from climbing the stairs, Uncle Sol went back down to his room.

There we were, Charlie, Elizabeth, and I, in front of the house, silent in the wake of the woodchuck's scurry across the lawn. "Before we leave tomorrow, I should at least try to block up that hole under the porch," I said after a minute or two.

"You wouldn't do it right, you know," Elizabeth said.

"I know, and it will only be a holding action, like everything else. But think of the pleasure Sol will get when I do it all wrong."

Charlie, on straight arms and legs, made his way over the grass. He clambered up the two steps to the porch, crawled to the door, stood up against it, and glanced back at us. He wanted to go inside and, I suspect, look for the old man.

Continuing Care

Somehow, Uncle Sol weathered another winter in his apartment in New York and made it back up here to the Berkshires. I've arranged for a visiting nurse to stop by his farmhouse three times a week and for a part-time housekeeper to come and clean and cook. Right now, though, Uncle Sol is in the hospital, over in Great Barrington. I'm taking my son, Charlie, two years old today—Saturday—to see him at about three this afternoon, and then we'll come back in time for Charlie's birthday party. Day before yesterday, on one of my solo visits, I asked Uncle Sol if it would be all right to hold the party at his house in his absence. His house, if it's still standing, will be my house someday, according to the new will Uncle Sol made a few years ago, after a decade of what I thought was deliberate tantalizing, which took one of two forms: You wouldn't want this place, Davey—it's too much to keep up, or, Won't you be happy knowing young Communists are going to camp here? I'm still not quite sure why he had a change of heart. Yes, I am. Elizabeth, my wife, won it.

"Go ahead, take the place over before I'm even cold in my grave," he said in reply to my request about Charlie's party. He had been feeling lousy and, I think, frightened all summer, and his customary mordant humor had been further darkened by sarcasm and intimations of mortality. After giving his consent, Uncle Sol informed me that he planned to be out of the hospital by Saturday anyway. I reminded him that his doctors said Monday at the earliest. "So that they can get even richer," he said. Elizabeth and Charlie and I are spending our vacation in a rented cottage about two miles from Uncle Sol's, down on William's Lake. It's close enough for us to be able to keep an eye on the old man and far enough to allow us to maintain an illusion of independence, but it doesn't have enough tradition or lawn for the dauphin's natal festivities. That's why I asked Uncle Sol if we could use his place.

At this very moment—noon—I am high up on a ladder that I've set against what used to be the horse barn at Uncle Sol's. I put a couple of thumbtacks through one end of a long, coiled red streamer, stick them into the side of the barn, and throw the coil so that as half of it unwinds in flight it arcs over the tall mock-orange bush to my right. The remainder lands in the middle of the lawn, between the dilapidated old barn and the dilapidated old house. A foot lower, I do the same thing with a blue streamer, and, lower still, another red one. At the K Mart in Great Barrington this morning, I decided that blue and red were Charlie's colors—blue for his eyes and red for the fact that it was the only other color the store had in stock. To make it easier to raise the bottom streamer a bit, I pull the ladder to me and put it back a few inches to the right—I feel like I'm Lindying with it. Something buzzes in my hair. I guess that even someone in his forties is looking rich in hemoglobin to the insects at Uncle Sol's. Their usual fare consists of my cousin Ella, who is in her mid-nineties, and who made it through the winter in the city in good enough shape to take her usual two months at Uncle Sol's, and Uncle Sol himself, who will turn ninety later this month. Slim pickings for little mandibles. Ella is up in her room, peering out at me as I teeter around on the ladder under the fiery-hot August sun. She's all screened in. And, of course, Uncle Sol is in the hospital. He had edema in his chest—a pleural effusion, the resident called it —and a touch of pneumonia. A surgeon tapped his chest and removed nearly a quart of fluid.

I bang the final thumbtack home with the heel of my hand, and I hear another buzz of wings, near my ear, and then something brushes the nape of my neck like a tiny piece of silk. I bat one hand about my head, and what I hit feels far more substantial than a mosquito or a horsefly. I look up and see fat, iridescent carpenter bees tumbling like paratroopers out of holes in the wood above me, just under the apex of the roof. I clamber down the ladder and jump the last three rungs—a feat that would have been nothing for me four years ago, but now my knees take instant and sharp exception to it—and run down the driveway. The bees peel off after about twenty feet. It's too hot out here even for them.

I go back up the driveway, remove the ladder from the side of the barn, carry it across the lawn, and prop it—carefully, just in case—against the woodshed end of the house. I pick up the streamer coils and climb the ladder and finish the job. The streamers look terrific—a red-and-blue gateway to the green expanse beyond, on which I've already set a wood trestle table from the farmhouse porch. On top of the table I've tacked down a white paper tablecloth with colorful cartoons of "Sesame Street" characters on its borders, and I've put eight bentwood chairs around the table. Uncle Sol has *thirty-three* bentwood chairs altogether. I counted them once, last spring, up in the attic, a couple of weeks before we drove Uncle Sol up to the house. Elizabeth followed me as I counted the chairs, saying, "Shame on you." I finished the count silently, and she asked me how many there were.

The chairs are for the eight kids, ranging in age from one to twelve, who will attend Charlie's party this afternoon. There will also be twenty-four adults—parents, grandparents, and friends, from neighboring houses and cottages down on the lake where our rented place is. Who are all these people? The oldest generation, most of them in their sixth or seventh decade, poured out of New York on spring, summer, and fall weekends during the Lefty heydays of the forties and fifties to visit Uncle Sol. They knew him from his work for the *Daily World* and from the settlement house he ran. Sol was the most social of socialists, with his square-dance calling and his vast repertoire of party games and his romantic and companionable version of Marxism. The young people who thronged to his place in the Berkshires fell in love with it, and as they grew older and money modified their politics, many of them bought land and houses in the neighborhood. They had children, who are now mainly in their thirties and are surprisingly liberal for their era and income bracket, and they hung around these hills a lot, too, and now those children are having children of their own. There's a bleeding heart or two at the end of most of the little dirt roads hereabouts. This summer is the first time in years that I've seen much of them, because it's the first time in years that I've been in the vicinity for more than a weekend or two. They haven't had much to do with Uncle Sol recently, either—they stop by, pay their respects, bring him and Ella a casserole, but they go away again pretty quickly. The place is a depressing shadow of its former self, with Uncle Sol clinging to his own existence by a thread spun out of good DNA, stubbornness, and fear. Anyway, sooner or later just about everybody has what he thinks of as a life of his own. I'll probably have one myself someday.

Four days ago, on Tuesday, I walked up from our cottage to see Uncle Sol during Charlie's noontime nap. He had been telling me all summer that we ought to have a talk about the things I would need to know when I inherited his place. That wasn't it at all, of course. He just wanted attention, as I came to realize after making a few attempts to prize from him at least one of the things I needed to know. "Not now," he would say. Or, "You just can't wait, can you?" Last Tuesday, after yet another such deferment, I noticed that he was shivering, even though he was sitting on the porch in his rocking chair in the full sun and had on begrimed wool trousers, a flannel shirt, a plaid wool jacket, and a baseball cap. His hands stuck out of the oversize jacket sleeves, quaking like bare twigs in a strong wind. His nose and ears, the only parts of him that seem not to have lost weight over the last few years, looked like galleon sails on a dinghy. I asked him if he was feeling all right.

"What kind of question is that, Davey?" he said. "You know how miserable I've been."

"I meant are you feeling worse. You're shivering."

"I'm afraid of what you might be planning to do to me."

"No, really."

"Yes, really."

"Come on."

"It's nothing—I'm just old and cold," he said. "Why don't you let me alone?"

At that moment, Elizabeth drove up the driveway with Charlie in back in his car seat. We had planned to go to Friendly's for lunch, over near the K Mart mall. "Your wish is my command," I said to Uncle Sol. "We're off to town."

"That's right—ten minutes of conversation and then leave me here to rot."

"It's more like an hour, Sol," I said. "And I can't stay with you and let you alone at the same time."

"You and your logic," he said. "Anyway, the kid there isn't as eager to get away from me as some others I might mention. He'll want to stick around a few minutes."

He was right. Charlie has formed an affection for Uncle Sol and the farmhouse which supersedes even his affection for fast food. "Want to get down!" I could hear him shouting from inside the car. "Want to see Uncle Sol. Want to see him."

Elizabeth lifted Charlie out of the car seat, and he was running when he hit the ground, his diaper making him look chunky under his blue shorts, like the halfback that everyone assures me he is going to grow up to become. He scrambled up onto the porch and embraced the old man's knees. Then, crying, "Lawnmower! Big lawnmower!," he took Uncle Sol's hand and tried to pull him up out of the rocking chair he was sitting in.

"All right, all right," Uncle Sol said. "Just let me get my cane, will you? You're like your father—always in a hurry."

"Can't you give it a rest?" I said.

"Why, Davey—I'm surprised at you," Uncle Sol said. "You know I'm only joking." He struggled up out of the rocker, took the cane from where he had hung it on the chair's back, and allowed himself to be hauled out behind the horse barn toward the rickety old shed that provides a long-defunct tractor mower, in whose sprung seat Charlie loves to sit, with the imperfect shelter it deserves. I resigned myself to an extra fifteen minutes of lunchlessness.

"What a picture," Elizabeth said just before Charlie, tugging away at Uncle Sol as if he were unsatisfied with merely psychological disarmament, and Uncle Sol, listing and shaking, hove beyond view. "It's like something out of Norman Rockwell."

"If you didn't know better," I said.

"Don't you think you overreacted a little?"

"It's just that he never gives me any credit—just wisecracks. No, you're right. And I was thinking as I was walking up here before, if it wasn't for Sol, Charlie wouldn't be getting homemade sugar cookies from Florrie Segal, and we wouldn't know the Simons or the Lipsons or the Bluesteins."

"He must have been like a human magnet," Elizabeth said.

I sat down on the porch rail, and Elizabeth took the vacant rocking chair. "So what's been happening up here?" she said.

"Overreaction and respiration, and that's about it," I said. "How was Charlie's nap?"

"Fine. More than an hour."

"Did you get any work done?" Elizabeth had said that she was going to begin transcribing an interview she'd had with a sleep expert, for an article about people who were preoccupied with their slumber or lack thereof. She's a free-lance journalist.

"No, I was too sleepy," she said.

Cicadas sawed away in the heat. Stones lay whitely in the driveway. My hands were at the ends of my arms.

"The Berkshires certainly are hopping this afternoon," Elizabeth said. She kicked off one of her imitation Topsiders and wiggled her foot at me. I kicked off one of my loafers and put my foot up against hers. "Sole mates," she said.

Ella opened the screen door and emerged from the house. Her outfit was a little crazy—running shoes, checked slacks, a striped blouse—but, with her calm demeanor and the strict bun of white hair at the back of her head, she could confer dignity on a clown costume. She had five horse-pill vitamins on a dinner plate in one hand and writing paper and envelopes in the other. She maintains an incredibly wide correspondence of the weather-report-and-health-status variety. "What's this?" she said, motioning toward our feet. "How are you two? It's getting hot. Where's the kid? Not in the sun, I hope." She started walking over to the trestle table and, about ten years later, sat down on one of the thirty-three bentwoods.

"You're right," I said to Elizabeth, reinstalling my foot in my shoe. "Sometimes the pace is just too much."

"What?" Ella said. "Oh, there he is." She raised her hand as if it weighed a hundred pounds and pointed it toward the horse barn. Charlie was cavorting more or less in our direction.

"Meat now," he called.

"Look at him," Ella said. "Isn't he something? What's he saying?"

"He wants his lunch," I said loudly.

"What a *fresser!*" Ella said. "He's definitely a *fresser.*"

Uncle Sol, gray as slate, tottered into sight.

"Sol looks awful," Ella said serenely.

"He really does," Elizabeth said. "Is he O.K.?"

"What?" Ella said.

"I asked him, because he was shivering, but he said he was all right," I said.

"What?" Ella said.

"Maybe he should go in with us and see the doctor," Elizabeth said.

"Maybe we should take him at his word," I said.

"Will someone please tell me what is going on?" Ella pleaded.

I turned to her and said, "Nothing—I swear to you, absolutely nothing."

"Thank God," she said. "Will you buy me a book of stamps if you go into town?"

Uncle Sol and his condition nagged at me for the rest of Tuesday—as I laughed at Charlie when he said, again and again on the way to the restaurant, "Shall we have lunch now? Sure!"; as we drove back to our cottage, with Elizabeth saying that the tall lilacs in front of Uncle Sol's should be cut back a little, for the sake of the view, me saying peremptorily, "I'll think about it when the time comes," Elizabeth replying, "Can't I even fantasize?," and Charlie issuing his standard orders for arguments between his mother and father ("No TALKING!"); as we went swimming among the weeds in William's Lake, with Charlie imploring me to jump off the dock backward and then crying in apprehension when I did so; as I performed my own ludicrously relaxed version of the seriously outdated Royal Canadian Air Force exercises while Elizabeth read to Charlie; as I started the charcoal in the barbecue grill; as we ate spareribs, corn, and tomatoes; as

Elizabeth gave Charlie his bath, with him crowing, "Noisy Charlie, noisy Charlie"; as darkness drew on and Elizabeth gave Charlie his one and only bottle of the day, which he shook every now and then, like a graffiti artist with a can of Krylon; and as Charlie drifted off to sleep, assuming the position of a Muslim in prayer and burrowing his lovely blond head under his cotton blanket, to the accompaniment, from me, of "Joe Hill," a song that Uncle Sol sang to me when I was a kid. I know, I know. If there were a word like "uxorious" that described certain kinds of fathers, that would be me. But I do my best to keep Charlie from realizing it.

"I'm never voting for one of these guys again," Elizabeth said. She was reading in the standard-issue summer-cottage armchair. The dishes were done, the toys picked up, the moon and stars out. I was on the similarly time-worn sofa, staring unproductively at a yellowed *Times Magazine* crossword puzzle from 1978, which I had found in a stack of papers near the fireplace, and reflecting that Uncle Sol always thinks he's sick when he's not and never does when he is, and that the visiting nurse I'd set up for him wouldn't be coming again until Friday. "They've taken so many risks with other people's lives!"

"Who?" I said.

"The Kennedys."

"What about them?"

"I'm never voting for one of them again."

"Why not?"

"This book is so scandalous."

"It's about the Kennedys?"

"Listen, I can tell you've been worrying about him," Elizabeth said. "You'd better drive up there and check on him."

I did.

"You again?" Ella said to me when I walked into Uncle Sol's living room. She was addressing an envelope. "How's the kid?

Sleeping? He didn't get a sunburn, I hope. He's something. Sol has been in bed since you left. I made him some Progresso soup, but he wouldn't take any. Have you ever tried it?"

"It's too salty for Uncle Sol—he shouldn't have it," I said.

"He's still in there," Ella said, gesturing toward Uncle Sol's room. "You'd better check on him."

Uncle Sol was dozing on his narrow bed. The forty-watt bulb in the overhead light fixture was dimly pinching pennies. I felt Uncle Sol's forehead. It was very hot. He awoke with a start. "I thought I got rid of you once and for all," he said feebly. On every second or third breath, he gave a faint dry cough.

I took his temperature. A hundred and four degrees. "You've got to go to the hospital," I said. "Do you feel up to going in with me, or should I call an ambulance?"

"And waste poor people's tax money?" Uncle Sol said, finding strength in indignation. "I should say not."

As I was helping Uncle Sol into the car, Ella came out to the driveway and tapped me on the shoulder. She handed me a sheaf of letters, saying, "Would you mind mailing these for me, if you go past the post office?"

Wasn't it selfish to buy such a small car, Uncle Sol asked me on the way—there wasn't much room to give anyone else a ride when Elizabeth and Charlie were along. Did I have to show off by driving so fast? It didn't look to him like I'd made a full stop back there at the stop sign. It would be better to keep my lights on low beam in town.

"Uncle!" I said as we pulled in—too sharply, for Uncle Sol —to the emergency-room entrance at the hospital.

"What?"

"I'm crying it. I give up."

The nurse on duty took Uncle Sol to an examination cubicle and left me in the waiting room. I spent the time looking at some rifle magazine that is an official publication of the N.R.A., and found myself fascinated by the ads for high-calibre weapons and bullets that explode on impact. Ten minutes of fantasy violence passed, and then the nurse came back out to ask me some questions that Uncle Sol couldn't remember the answers to. "He told me that you're his grandfather," she said uncertainly. "He's a very sweet and intelligent man, isn't he?"

A little while later, after I'd called Elizabeth on the pay phone to tell her where I was and what was going on, a wispy-bearded resident who looked all of seventeen came out and beckoned me into the emergency room's interior. Uncle Sol was lying flat on his back on a gurney, dozing once again. The sight of him so frail and ashen took away the anger I was feeling, but for an instant I resented him even for that. The resident showed me a chest X-ray clipped up over a light box at the back of the cubicle. He explained about the fluid on Uncle Sol's lungs, and he said he probably had pneumonia, and would have to be in the hospital for a week after his chest was drained. The X-ray, with its charcoal-gray spaces bridged by white bars and shrouded in vaporous white mists, looked sepulchral—like a still of death itself.

The resident turned off the light box and drew me outside the cubicle. He closed the curtain in front of it and tugged sagely on a strand or two of his beard. "Has Sol ever expressed any wishes concerning heroic measures if they should be necessary to keep him alive?" he asked. "Talking to him, he didn't seem to be the kind of person who would want that."

"I've never discussed the matter with my uncle," I said. "But I don't think he would want any pointless treatment." Then it came home to me what was being discussed. "Why—do you think he's dying?"

"No, no, I wouldn't say that, no. I think he'll probably respond to the medication and removal of the fluid and recover from this particular episode. But, between you and I, he is of a certain age, and, as far as treatment, it might be advisable to know his wishes."

.   .   .

[95]

When I went to visit Uncle Sol Wednesday afternoon, his temperature had come down a couple of degrees, and he was feeling better—well enough to chastise me for having brought him there "when it was completely unnecessary." Thursday was the day I asked him if it was all right to have Charlie's party at his place and he accused me of wanting him out of the way. "And speaking of illness," I said, ignoring the charges against me, partly because they were ridiculous and partly because they weren't, "I want to ask you something that I'm asking only because I don't have to. If I had to ask it, I wouldn't ask it."

"Enough riddles."

"If you got really sick and could be kept alive only by extreme measures—if you were in an irreversible coma, say—what would you want me to tell the doctors?"

"Absolutely not," he said. "It's criminal what they do to people now for no reason. It's horrible, and it costs a great deal of money."

"I thought you'd say that."

"But wait a minute. There are some things I have to tell you before you seal my coffin—the things about the house, and some other things, about myself."

"What things?" I asked. "I know about the drug ring and the white-slaving."

"I'm too tired to talk about it now. Besides, it looks like we have company."

A thin middle-aged woman wearing a loose-fitting white nurse's smock had come into the room. "I'm from Continuing Care," she said, and she looked it—pale, worried, a furrow in her brow. "Will your father be needing any help when he leaves the hospital?" I thanked her and told her that my father and I had things at home pretty well arranged, and that news, I was glad to see, seemed to cheer her up considerably.

On Friday evening, Uncle Sol was asleep when I arrived, and before I went to the cafeteria for a cup of coffee I stood in his doorway for a few minutes. He was the only patient in a double room on the third floor, and his bed was near the window, with a view of the Berkshires rolling off toward the east. It was warm outside, as it had been all week, but it was cool in the hospital, and the treetops were comically green and perfect—like thousands of broccoli heads. Uncle Sol's face was turned toward the window, and all I could see of it was one large ear, one sharp, gaunt cheekbone, and the fore section of that formidable nose, which had steered him in so many risky and romantic directions over his ninety years—from the trenches in the Argonne to the bleak hills around Madrid, and from there to a sometimes even more frightening battle against the Red-baiters and crypto-Fascists in this country in the middle of the century. I had seen that he was asleep, but from the door he looked as if he were waiting for the night to fall, as if something that would arrive with the darkness might take him on the most frightening journey of all. I thought, How awful to have done so much and now be able to do nothing. And then I left him alone.

When I went back, twenty minutes later, he was awake, and the young resident was there, folding his stethoscope and putting it into the side pocket of his white coat with crisp professionalism. "The data from this morning's lab tests isn't in yet," he said, "but we are showing definite signs of improvement, aren't we, Sol?"

As he left the room, Uncle Sol and I joined forces in an angry glare. Then he turned to me and said, "It's about time you came to visit me."

"Sol, I've been here every day."

"I thought you inherited your long nose from our family—now I know better."

"But I have—you just don't remember. You're probably not all the way awake yet."

"I wasn't sleeping," he said. "Where's the boy?"

"He's taking his nap, back at the cottage."

"You probably let him sleep as much as he wants."

"You said it."

"Well, I want to see him."

"You'll see more of him than you want to when you get home."

"Tell me again who's going to be at this shindig."

"Well, there's the Segals—"

"Oh, yes, he's the one who built the fancy-schmancy house near our place."

"—and their daughter and granddaughter, and the Kurlands—"

"Oh, I remember when that fellow What's-His-Name was a decent, modest guy, but now . . ."

"And the Simons and their grandson—"

"He used to visit all the time, you know," Uncle Sol said. "It's hard to believe that he was once a good radical. Well, it will take me just a few minutes to get ready." He got himself up into a sitting position.

"What are you doing?" I said.

"I'm going to get dressed and go back with you to the party, of course."

No, Uncle Sol, I say, it's evening, and the party isn't until tomorrow. And you have to stay here until Monday. I've been telling you that all along. Yes, I have. Yes, I have been here before. I brought you in, and I've visited three days in a row. No, I'm not trying to put something over on you. You're just groggy from sleeping. I saw you. No, it wasn't someone else. No, there's nothing wrong with my eyes. Yes, maybe you should lie down again. I'm sorry you're feeling weak.

On second thought, Uncle Sol, I say to myself, maybe you would like to step over to the window for a few minutes. When I drove in, there was a little fire smoldering in the dumpster at the end of the parking lot, and if you lean out the window far enough you might just be able to see it. I know it isn't much in the way of excitement, but. . . . What? You can't make it out? Here, let me help you.

As I gave Elizabeth my exasperated report on the visit over dinner, Charlie, who had been deprived of Uncle Sol's company for three days, relentlessly interjected, "Want to see Uncle Sol? Sure! *I* drive! *I* drive!" After I finished and Charlie stopped explaining to us that Uncle Sol was in the hospital because he was sick, and stopped repeating his entreaties to see him, and made the last of his offers of chauffeur services, Elizabeth said, "It really is a shame that he won't be able to go to the party."

"Well, I'll at least take Charlie in to see him tomorrow," I said. "Right now, what I'm thinking is they can have each other."

I'm all finished with the decorating. I've wrapped the porch railings with twisted streamers, hung a "Happy Birthday" sign over the door into the house, and stashed little bags of party favors in hiding places near the lawn—some obscure, for the older kids, and some in nearly plain sight, for the younger ones. One bag is on the seat of the big desuetudinous mower. At the party I'll whisper to Charlie that he should go and take a look. The sun is just settling down behind the treetops, and the lawn is in shadow—it will be perfect for the party. I'm sitting in the living room, drinking a can of truly loathsome generic diet strawberry soda from the case that Uncle Sol had me buy on sale at the beginning of the summer as a concession to his sweet tooth. "You're a fine young man," I suddenly remember Uncle Sol saying to me from his rocker as he watched me lug the twenty-four cans of chemicals up onto the porch. "Not so young," I said. "You are a fine young man," he said. "You've been a great help to me. Don't ever think that I don't appreciate it." I would like to say that I looked him square in the eye and told him I loved him, or that I put my burden down and embraced him, but I can't. I pretended to have trouble opening the screen door, mumbled, "Thanks," and beat it inside the house. He's not the only one with a communication problem, I guess. "So don't be so hard on him," I say out loud, though no one's here.

Ella descends from her room in party finery, looking ancient and lovely. "Hello, Mister," she says as she sits down at her writing desk—an old typewriter table that Uncle Sol found on the street in New York just before the War of 1812 broke out. "Where are your wife and son? Staying cool, I hope. He's something. I saw you running up and down the ladder. It's too hot for that kind of work." She bends to her epistolary tasks. The house is quiet and cool, and I feel that I should just keep sitting here for a few minutes—that when Ella took her place at her shabby escritoire some sort of symmetry came into being, a pattern or a picture was completed, with Uncle Sol waiting for Charlie's visit forming part of it, with Charlie and Elizabeth, whom I suddenly find myself actively and almost painfully loving, down in the cottage forming another part, with me forming a definitely ancillary one, and with Ella, of all people, at the center, maybe because it is Ella who sends out the dispatches, however dry, from here to the world at large. And I feel that if I move too quickly it will break up the composition before it has a chance to—to register. In other words, I say to myself, to dispel all these metaphysical vapors, you're happy.

"I'm so embarrassed I could *die!*" one young nurse says to another in the hospital elevator, as they get off at the floor below the one Uncle Sol is on.

"Die," says Charlie, testing the unfamiliar word.

"Let's talk about something else," I say, as the elevator doors open and we get off, but I'm grinning, and Charlie can see it. In front of us, near the nurses' station, happens to be the tufty resident, looking soulful as ever.

"Die," says Charlie.

The resident regards us with baffled consternation. "I'm sorry," he says. "We did everything we could, but it was no use."

"What happened?" I say.

"Die," Charlie says, uncertainly, sensing trouble in the air.

"We did our best, but—"

"Oh, my God," I say. I reach for Charlie's hand.

"He just wouldn't listen."

"What are you talking about?"

"He insisted on getting dressed and packing his things."

"You let him get dressed and he died?"

"Did someone die?"

"You just said—"

"What? Oh, no. I didn't mean to infer that. Your uncle. He insists on leaving the hospital. He wants to attend some party, he says. He signed the forms. Against medical advice. But we can't force him to stay here. He's ready to go."

More than ready to go, I see. Going. Uncle Sol is turning the corner of the elevator bank, his cane in one hand and his crummy leather overnight bag in the other, and with a kidney-shaped plastic dish filled with hospital freebies—toothbrush, toothpaste, baby powder, lotion—tucked under his arm. Charlie runs over to him and hugs his unsteady legs. "You're late," Uncle Sol says. "I've been waiting an hour."

The grass lot across the road from Uncle Sol's house is filled with cars. Uncle Sol insists that no one park in the driveway when he's around—it spoils the view of the lawn and outbuildings, he says—and even though the guests think he's not around, and even though they rarely visit, they've had years of training, and they follow this rule as if it were canon law. There are about twenty cars on the grass, and it's not easy to find a place to park. Then I have to help Uncle Sol out of the car and persuade him to leave his effects behind for the time being. Across the road, everyone is milling around at the top of the driveway, looking toward the porch—which, I notice, has fallen down rather seriously at one end since I saw it last, about an hour ago. I know it's silly—unbecoming, as Elizabeth would say—but I feel as if Charlie and I are about to be upstaged, as if all the guests somehow suddenly know that Uncle Sol has sprung himself, and are standing around waiting for him to step up on the good end of the porch and take a bow. Except Elizabeth, whose darling Charlie is and always will be, and who I think understands the toll all this is taking on me, even though we've never really talked about it.

Charlie holds my hand and Uncle Sol leans heavily on my other arm as we slowly make our way across the road and up the driveway. I feel like some crazy version of "The Spirit of '76." Elizabeth catches sight of us inching upward. "Uncle Sol!" she says. "Hey, here they are." Everyone turns to look at us, and a big cheer goes up. I decide to believe that some of the acclaim is for Charlie and me.

Last Lessons

NIGHT WAS COMING ON. Charlie—two and a half—was at the far end of the long, cluttered hall in our apartment, serenading a putty knife and a big pair of pliers from what we call, laughably, the utility closet. He had rejected his Playskool Workbench, as usual, and had wheedled the supposedly forbidden real tools out of me by supplicatory escalation. "I can see the tools?" "I can get closer?" "I can touch them?" "I can lift them up?"

I gave in, because I wanted the quarter hour of peace with the newspaper that surrender would guarantee. I'm forty-four years old, and having to make decisions about my Uncle Sol and to supervise his care up at his farmhouse in the Berkshires for the last three months have taken such a toll on me that I've come to believe I can physically feel the years eroding toward me from the end of my life, especially at three in the morning, when I wake up and wonder whether Uncle Sol is uncomfortable or lonely, or when I have to call one of his nurse's aides and ask her not to help herself to another aide's special tea bags, or when the spectre of his meagre financial resources rises up to haunt me.

It is the middle of December and unusually cold—so cold that yesterday I took the subway home from Columbia (where I teach journalism) instead of walking. When I opened the door, Charlie was right there, holding the contemptible Workbench. He dropped it and immediately started in with an unctuous "Why don't you take off your coat? Take off it." Elizabeth, my wife, was in the kitchen. "Is that you, Dave?" she called. I'd like to be able to say that in walking down the hall to greet her I was drawn on by the aroma of something cooking, but no such luck. Elizabeth had been trying to finish an article about hostages for *Popular Psychology* during the five hours Charlie was with the babysitter, and she had been occupied with him after that.

"Chinese?" she said. She was standing at the kitchen counter, poring over takeout menus.

"Great," I said. She gave me a kiss—a real one.

"Chinese!" Charlie shouted from the hall, beginning to home in on the utility closet. "I can have dumplings? I can pay the man money?"

Forty-five minutes later we were sitting at the drop-leaf table in the dining room, eating dumplings and pineapple chicken and beef with snow peas out of cartons. The pliers lay beside Charlie's placemat, and a skirt of rice surrounded his chair.

"Did you finish the piece?" I asked Elizabeth.

"Barely," she said. "I finally got in touch with Ruth Paris, that psychologist I told you about. She says that hostages often regress so far that they begin to regard their captors as parents and—"

"More rice," Charlie said.

I cocked an eyebrow at him.

"Please!" he said.

"What's new with you?" Elizabeth said.

"The dean asked me if I'd like to go out to the Midwest in April to be on a panel at some journalism school," I said. "They're having their twenty-fifth anniversary."

"Maybe Charlie and I could go, too," Elizabeth said.

"It will just be for a couple of days."

"Where we going?" Charlie said.

"Well, Dad may have to go away for a couple of days, but not for a long time," I said.

"What?" Charlie said.

"It's in Kansas or Missouri or somewhere," I said. "Anyway, it's a state, the way New York is a state. New York is a city, too, but you don't have to worry about any of that."

"What?" Charlie said. He looked at me in utter bewilderment. Then his face brightened, and he said, "It has tools?"

The telephone in the kitchen rang, and Elizabeth got up to answer it. "It's for you," she said. "Dr. Reilly."

Uncle Sol's doctor up in Sheffield.

Uncle Sol had to go into the hospital in Great Barrington four times during August, September, and October, to have the fluid that kept accumulating around his lungs removed. The last two times, he almost didn't recover from the procedure. The fluid was the result of congestive heart failure—a condition he had had for years but one that up until last summer had been controlled with digitalis. Just after he reached ninety, his tough old heart had begun to give out in an irremediable way, and his kidneys started to fail. "The old gentleman is in his last days" is how Dr. Reilly put it.

Dr. Reilly was a general practitioner, who had taken over from a bearded resident the third time Uncle Sol was hospitalized. The resident called Dr. Reilly in for a consultation, and he and Uncle Sol got on like a couple of old shipmates—which was surprising, since Dr. Reilly, I learned, was a devout Catholic with six sons and three daughters, a Republican, and a rich man, and Uncle Sol was a devout atheist, a bachelor, a Communist, and . . . well, Uncle Sol. In early September, in handling Uncle Sol's mail, I came across a mailing-list invitation to a "Salute Dr. Kevin

Reilly Day" at Pittsfield General Hospital. I asked a storekeeper in Sheffield about him and was told, "Oh, he's a great man. Everybody in Berkshire County knows him. He was born right here in Sheffield seventy-some years ago, you know. Oh, everybody just loves him." At first it seemed strange that Uncle Sol had chosen as an aide-de-camp for what was probably his last stand a man so different from him, but, then, as I reminded myself, Uncle Sol had had a lifetime of taking on odd recruits.

"At some point he will drift into a uremic coma and then just slip away from us," Dr. Reilly went on to explain about Uncle Sol's prognosis. "It is by no means the worst way to go." Dr. Reilly and I were standing in the living room of Uncle Sol's farmhouse. It was about two on a bright, chilly November Saturday. That morning, I had left Elizabeth and Charlie in our apartment, in Charlie's room, building an elaborate and fanciful version of Uncle Sol's place—which Charlie had come to love during the summer—out of Lego blocks. Having decided that the farmhouse was also a zoo and a gas station, Charlie was trying to force a flexible plastic straw into the mouth of a little toy lion. "It needs gas," he said, wriggling away from my kiss. Elizabeth had offered her own and Charlie's company on the trip, but I didn't think Charlie would go for so much driving. Anyway, it wasn't a recreational trip: I was going up to visit Uncle Sol, to decide whether the deteriorating old house could be kept warm and comfortable enough for the deteriorating old man as the winter drew on, and to talk to Dr. Reilly about his condition.

Dr. Reilly had asked me to call him from Uncle Sol's, but when I walked into the house, there he was, sitting in the red wing chair at the table in the living room, looking at an old family photograph album of Uncle Sol's. I was pasted in it somewhere, standing on Uncle Sol's shoulders about forty years ago. And Uncle Sol was in there at about four, too, standing on his father's shoulders at the turn of the century, in front of a textile factory in Elizabeth, New Jersey, the considerable profits from which my

grandfather shared equally—communistically—with his employ-
ees. Sunlight streamed in the window and over Dr. Reilly's slightly
stooped shoulders as he studied the album. He started a bit when
I cleared my throat to let him know I was there.

"Dave," he said. "I dropped by to see the old fellow on this
beautiful day, and then Sarah said you were coming up, so I
thought I might wait for a while." He got up to shake hands, his
ruddy face beaming with Irish heartiness. Stooped shoulders and
all, he was six-six if he was an inch. "Sarah is in there giving our
friend an alcohol rub-down," he said, nodding toward Uncle Sol's
bedroom.

"How is he doing?"

"The same, really."

"It's incredibly nice of you to make a house call on Saturday,"
I said.

"Well, I missed him. And, you know, I was over here a couple of weeks ago, just after Sol got out of the hospital, and I liked
the place. It's very peaceful. The view from the driveway is lovely.
I feel at home here."

"Still, you must be busy," I said. "I know Sol appreciates
your coming out here. He thinks you're something."

"I am, I really am," Dr. Reilly said.

Sarah Deane, one of the nurse's aides who had been staying
with Uncle Sol twenty-four hours a day since October, at a cost
of about a thousand dollars a week, came out of his room. Sarah
wore bright colors for a woman in her sixties, and I had hired
her for her general, although sometimes clinical, sunniness. There
seemed to be hundreds of kind women in the Berkshire Hills
looking for this sort of work. I'd interviewed ten, chosen six, and
set up shifts and backups. I'd also rented a hospital bed and a
walker and a home oxygen system. Uncle Sol had enough money
left to go on like that for not much more than four months, as I
had every reason to know, since I spent about an hour a day in
the city sending checks up to Massachusetts and keeping his rec-

ords straight. During the interviews, I'd asked each applicant if she would mind staying with Uncle Sol if he was actually dying. Sarah had replied, "Oh, no—I love terminal." She greeted me cheerfully now and said that she had finished the rub-down and that I could go in and see Uncle Sol.

"Just one more minute of your time," Dr. Reilly said to me. "You know, Dave, he isn't quite the same, really." And it was then that he went into the medical detail and said that Uncle Sol didn't have much longer to go. "A month, maybe two," he said in conclusion. "I don't think there will be any point in any heroic treatment. He told me last summer that he didn't want things prolonged senselessly. I know you're wondering about keeping him here, and I don't want to interfere, but I would welcome the chance to come out and see him from time to time."

Where else was I going to find that kind of attention for Uncle Sol? If the furnace gave out or the electrical system blew or the house just plain fell down, he could always go back to the hospital or to a nursing home, or even to his apartment in New York, in an ambulance. If it was O.K. with him, he would stay right here, surrounded by his Reginald Marsh drawings and Mexican rugs, the incomprehensible old board games and scratched 78s stuffed into cupboards, the squirrels in the walls and the mice in the pantry, the sounds of the old house trying to keep out the bitter winds of yet another winter. And the ministrations of these country people, who seemed to regard him as a gentleman from another, older, somehow more impressive world. There appeared to be more respect for age in the country than in the city, and more room for dying.

"He's wandering a little today," Sarah told me. "The way he did when you called on Wednesday and Gloria was here. She said he ordered you to come up and paint the front hall."

"He might have done the same thing even if his head was clear," I said.

"I know, I know," Sarah said. "At least he got rid of that gas that was on his intestine yesterday."

Dr. Reilly said goodbye, and I went into Uncle Sol's room and stood next to his bed. His eyes were closed. He had lost so much weight that there might have been nothing more than kindling under the covers. The skin on his bald head was taut and dry, as if it had undergone a curing process, and his ears and nose looked bigger than ever—elephantine. A clear plastic tube with two openings at the end, just under his cavernous nostrils, carried oxygen to him from the large cannister under the high night table at his bedside. The faint hiss and bubbling of the oxygen through a bottle of distilled water on the cannister's side sounded like rain approaching.

"Uncle Sol, I'm here," I said.

"No need to shout," he said weakly.

"Sorry."

"You always were a noisy brat," he said. "Father couldn't stand it sometimes. He would have to leave the house."

"Sol, you're thinking of your brother Joe—my father. I'm Dave."

He peered closely at me. "Why, so you are. Oh, Davey, you must think I'm a senile old eejit."

"No more than usual."

His eyes closed, and there was silence in the room. Then he said, "I'm so sorry about Nick's death. He was such a fine guy."

Nick was my brother. He died of septicemia after routine knee surgery when we were both in our twenties.

"That was a long time ago," I said. "Nineteen sixty-seven."

"Really?" Uncle Sol said. "It seems like yesterday."

"Sometimes it seems that way to me, too."

"He turned sorta conservative for a while after law school, you know," Uncle Sol said. "But I brought him around about that war over in wherever it was."

"Vietnam."

"Yes, Vietnam."

"Well, um, with all due respect, Sol, I think Nick pretty much brought himself around on that."

"You never heard the conversations we had," he said. "You're talking a lot of bulldozers, as usual."

I couldn't have heard the conversations, because you didn't have them, I thought, but this time I held my tongue.

"Listen, I didn't come up here to argue with you," I said.

"Are you sure?"

"I thought we should talk about whether you want to stay here, assuming you're going to need medical attention for a while. I could try to arrange things so that you could go back to the city. I wouldn't mind at all."

"I have a great deal to do there, naturally," Uncle Sol said. "The people at the *Daily World* always need all the volunteer help they can get. And I should be looking after Ella." Ella is a ninety-four-year-old cousin of ours who has always spent her summers at Uncle Sol's and lives during the winter in a housing project in New York, and if anyone would look after anyone, it would be the other way around. "But to tell you the truth, Davey, I'm feeling too punk to travel, so I think I'd better stick around here —at least for the time being."

"O.K., fine—I hoped you would say that."

"So you won't have to think about me, isn't that so, boy? So I'll be off your mind."

"Charlie will miss seeing you in New York," I said.

"Still spoiling him?" Uncle Sol said. He knitted his brow.

"Are you in any pain?" I asked.

"No," he said very quietly.

"You don't hurt anywhere?"

"No"—a little more loudly. "Ask me again and I'll tell you the same."

"Are you afraid?"

He looked at me in puzzlement. "Of what?" he said.

"Oh, I don't know. All these strangers coming and going—that kind of thing."

"Dr. Whosis is no stranger."

"Reilly."

"Yes. He's a good man—just a little misguided in some ways. He can learn a lot from me. The only thing I'm afraid of is that you're going to hang around here and not let me get my rest."

Nevertheless, as I left Uncle Sol's room I changed my plans and decided to spend the night, partly for Uncle Sol's sake and partly because I wanted to. Like Dr. Reilly, I found it calm there at the farmhouse. Sarah and her colleagues, with time on their hands, had made the place as neat as such a jumbled depository could be. It was a house that, like a church, had—at least for now—only one function, that was free of strollers and tricycles and bags of groceries and briefcases and phone books open on the couch, and free, too, of the cross-purposes of lives lived under the pretense of ignorance of their ending.

Sarah was sitting in the living room in the red wing chair, where Dr. Reilly had been when I arrived. She was working on a vivid needlepoint motto, and the concentration involved gave her ordinary looks dignity. The sun was low, drawing a line across the middle of the trees outside the window, with everything above the line as brilliant as flame in its reds and yellows and everything below sombre, almost obscure. I told Sarah that I'd decided to stay until the morning.

"What a fine idea," she said. "It will mean a lot to him. He thinks the world of you, you know."

"You and the others are taking such good care of everything around here," I said. "I think he's just going to stay on—he seems to want to."

"We *were* wondering about how long our jobs would last," Sarah said. "With Christmas coming and all that."

"I guess they'll last as long as he does."

"And that may be for a good long time yet, no matter what the doctor says. I didn't think he could live through that terrible sinus inflammation last week. Your uncle has a strong will, you know. And he's so very interesting."

There was nothing for me to do. I couldn't even call Elizabeth, because it was about four, and she'd be picking Charlie up at the babysitter's. So I put on my coat and went out of the house and took a walk in the last light up in the meadow behind Uncle Sol's. It came to me as I struggled up the hill how tired I was, how much I wanted the kind of help that only my brother could have given me, and in the middle of that lovely field, with the sun just catching the tops of the hills across the valley to the west and the yellow timothy nodding away around me at whatever the wind was saying, I cursed him silently for dying, and wished there was some way I could just walk away from everything.

When I went back down and called home a little later, Charlie picked up the phone before Elizabeth could get to it. "Charlie, let Mommy have that, please," I heard her say.

"I want it," he said.

"No, I have to answer it."

"You say no, I say yes," Charlie said coolly, just before Elizabeth wrested the receiver from him. That almost made me reconsider my decision to stay the night, but then I heard Charlie go crying loudly down the hall, and Elizabeth dropped the phone, and while she fumbled for it for a second, the peace at Uncle Sol's reasserted itself.

I had dinner in Great Barrington at a restaurant called Tiger Lily's, the most recent flower of the town's gentrification, but the season was between gentries right then, with summer people gone and skiers not yet arrived. Instead, there were a lot of beery hunters out from Boston, and as I ate at the bar I listened to them talk. They were having a good time.

In the morning, after a cup of coffee with Martha Scott, the aide who had come on at midnight, I stood once again at Uncle

Sol's bedside. We talked for half an hour or so—about small
things. The lateness of the fall this year. The old dictionary stand
in a corner of his room which he wanted me to sell because he
thought that one of the "gals" taking care of him could use the
money. The hermitlike ways of Fred Becker, the man who clears
the driveway of snow in the winter. They say he will shoot at
you if you go on his land. At one point, Uncle Sol began to tell
me a dream he'd had during the night, about playing Ping-Pong
outdoors with a rich woman whose butler picked up the ball
every time it fell to the ground. The account of the dream slowly
turned into a recollection of something he thought had actually
happened, and just the other day, at that, and then into plans to
receive the woman the following week, on the visit that Uncle
Sol had finally decided to permit her to pay him. I brought him
back to what passed for reality in that strange place, and he apol-
ogized for his confusion. I told him that it was all right, and that
I loved him. Just as he went back to sleep, I saw with delight,
outside one of his windows on the north side of the house, nine
or ten wild turkeys running across what used to be the vegetable
garden. The first rays of the sun made roads of light and shadow
for them, and they went clumsily along as if there were somewhere they had to be by the time the sun was all the way up. I
would have awakened Uncle Sol again just to point them out to
him, but I knew his eyes were too weak to see even half that far.

That is how it came about that Uncle Sol has remained up at his
farmhouse in the hills as the days shorten and he dwindles away
toward death. For more than a month now, I've been calling Dr.
Reilly twice a week, trying from a distance to settle disagree-
ments among the women who are taking care of Uncle Sol, urging friends of Uncle Sol's who were going up to their country
houses to visit him, phoning my cousin Ella to keep her posted
on Uncle Sol's condition, sending those enormous checks north-
ward on his behalf. I have had full power of attorney for Uncle

Sol for two years now. I can sign the checks "David Leonard (POA)" or just sign Uncle Sol's name. Elizabeth says that "POA" really stands for "Prisoner of Altruism." I point out to her that since I'll inherit Uncle Sol's place when he dies, I have no choice about helping him. She says I would do it anyway, but I'm not so sure. Maybe the person I am now would do it anyway, but would I be the person I am now if Uncle Sol hadn't announced some years back that he was leaving the place to me? Anyway, I always not only choose Uncle Sol's name for the check's bottom line but do my best to imitate his signature, as if I were desperate to be getting away with *something*.

Last night, when I got up from dinner to take Dr. Reilly's call, which could only be ominous, Elizabeth picked Charlie up off the booster seat, brushed the rice from his overalls, and hustled him away down the hall.

"Dr. Reilly, it's Dave," I said. "I guess something has happened."

"Well, the old gentleman seems to be going fast, I'm afraid. I'm out here at the house now, because Gloria gave me a call at home. Sol is unconscious and can't be roused, and his extremities are very cold. I don't think he can make it for more than another day or two, really, and it could well be much less than that, if his kidneys have shut down. I don't like disturbing you, but I thought you should know."

"Do you think I should go up now?" I asked.

"I can't answer that," Dr. Reilly said.

"Of course you can't. I'm sorry. Do you think he will last through the night?"

"He could fool us all. He fooled me twice last fall with that pleural effusion, and he doesn't seem to be in any discomfort now. I just can't say, really."

"It's good of you to come out at night," I said.

"Oh, I'm a great man, I am," Dr. Reilly said. "That's what they all tell me, at any rate. Dave, I'm going to go home now. If things take a sudden slide downhill, Gloria will call me again. Why don't you talk to her about your plans?"

"Let me think it over for a few minutes. I'll call her."

"I'll come out again tomorrow if he's still with us," Dr. Reilly said.

I found Elizabeth and Charlie in Charlie's room. "Shall we build a farmhouse?" he said when I came in. "Shall we build a zoo?" Between and in the middle of his invitations, which got steadily louder, I filled Elizabeth in, briefly and euphemistically, about what was going on up in the country. I said I thought I should go right away.

"This is beginning to get to me," she said. "I'm sorry, I care about Uncle Sol, too, but I can't help it."

"I want to see Uncle Sol," Charlie said. "I want to go to the farmhouse.",

"It's still a lot harder on me," I said. "I've kept it away from you and Charlie as much—"

"I wake up in the middle of the night when you do, you know."

"But it's all going to be over soon—"

"Shall we build a farmhouse?" Charlie implored.

"I really think I ought to—"

"Sometimes it seems as though you're almost using it to avoid things here."

"Don't be ridiculous," I said. "I wish he had you-knowed last summer, or five years ago, for Christ's sake."

"*I'm talking!*" Charlie shouted.

"Don't say that," Elizabeth said to me. "Look, just go up first thing in the morning. I'll call and cancel your classes for you."

"You'll have to share the guilt if he you-knows tonight."

Relieved and resentful, I hoisted Charlie up in my arms just as he was about to start crying in earnest. Elizabeth put her arm around us both and kissed me on the cheek.

"We're a family," Charlie said.

"If you say so," I said. "Let's go have our fortune cookies," and back down the hall we went. My fortune said "Society prepares the crime, the criminal commits it," and I couldn't help wondering whether the *Daily World* had gone into the fortune-cookie business. Elizabeth's said "You have the wisdom of the ages at your command." Charlie squinted at his little strip of paper and said, "I think I can know it."

I built a farmhouse, a zoo, and a museum with Charlie, gave him his bath, and read *The Cat in the Hat* to him three times, while Elizabeth wrapped presents in the living room. After he was asleep, I called Ella to tell her what was going on.

"Well, Mister, it's hard on you," Ella said when I was done with my report. "I'm glad to hear you're not racing up there tonight. Think of the cold, and it's supposed to snow, too. How's the boy? Well I hope. And Elizabeth? She's some gal. Oh, poor Sol. I'm glad he's not in pain. I wish there was something I could do to help. Well, so long."

And *that* is how it has come about that I am barrelling through Sharon, Connecticut, at 8 A.M. today instead of 8 P.M. yesterday. After a surprisingly sound sleep, I called the farmhouse at six this morning, and Sarah told me Uncle Sol was barely hanging on. "If only he would void," she said just before we hung up. "That would make me so happy." I feel as much in a race against time and conscience as I would have last night, but at least I don't have any guilt about leaving Elizabeth and Charlie behind this morning. When I got out of bed, Elizabeth said groggily that she thought they should come with me, but I could tell she didn't mean it.

Ella's snow held off until dawn. It started in New York just as I was pulling out of a precious parking spot in front of our house, but it remained light until I turned off Route 22 near Wassaic. There the wind began to swirl and the sky thickened, as if some rich frozen confection were being prepared by an unseen

hand above the hills. The grayness of the Harlem Valley, with its
cheesy motels and diners and malls and boarded-up farm stands
and, at Wingdale, its gigantic, ghastly red brick repositories for
the mentally ill, gave way just over the Connecticut border to
rolling countryside and a peaceful world of lovely farmland beginning its long winter rest. There are few cars on the road
now—every now and then I encounter a truck laden with Christmas trees heading south—and the tires of mine are quiet on the
snow. If Uncle Sol were with me, he would say, "What's your
rush, boy? You trying to finish me off? Why don't we stop for a
minute at that little place near Salisbury and get a bite?" And if
we did that, he would complain about the prices and stop just
short of refusing to allow me to pick up the check. He would talk
about the days when he called square dances at the Litchfield Hill
School, and about how sorry he felt for the boys who were having their values ruined by their rich parents. He would tell me
how I was spoiling Charlie, too, and then interrupt himself to ask
if I ever played the guitar for him. He would remind me of the
summer he taught me how to play. I was fifteen. "You were the
laziest thing I've ever seen," he would say. "You had a feeling
for music, and why you liked that rock-and-roll business I'll never
know. 'Here, learn something worthwhile,' I told you one day
and showed you a few chords. Do you remember what you said?
You said, 'I don't want to start on this, because I'll get interested
and then I'll have to work at it.' But you went ahead anyway—
I made you. And aren't you grateful now?" And, Sol, do *you*
remember the story you told me that same summer, after you
found me necking out in the barn with that girl, Jennifer, from
the cottage down on William's Lake? "Now, it's only natural that
you are interested in girls," you said. "But you have to be careful,
or it will ruin you. I knew a young man about your age once
who was a very promising singer. He was training for the opera.
But then he got involved with a gal, and he was much too young
for that. The whole business got the better of him, and it reached

the point where if he saw a pretty girl out in the audience when he was onstage he would get aroused and have to stop the performance. That's the kind of thing that can happen."

Tyranny, tyranny. Maybe not over my politics or my character, which is what he was aiming for—I'm only a little left of liberal and definitely this side of priapic—but certainly over a large portion of my memory, which ought to be dominion enough for anyone, and certainly for the rest of my life. Still—or therefore—I would like very much to have the chance to say goodbye to him, and I hope I make it in time. I hope I make it at all, what with this blanket of snow descending and the silly mistiness in my eyes.

Through Lakeville and along Under Mountain Road. Right on Berkshire School Road over to Sheffield. Then up into the hills to the east, swishing along over the snow, with only the thought of Charlie keeping me from being entirely reckless. Up the driveway and out of the car and up to my calves in whiteness as light as feathers. Sarah's car is here, and there's smoke coming out of the chimney. The quiet is complete, until I stamp the snow off my slacks and shoes on the porch.

Sarah greets me with "You won't believe this, and I don't believe it myself, but he has come back. He came to about two hours ago and said he was hungry. He ate a whole jar of that Gerber applesauce and two pieces of toast. Then he passed some water. I was never so glad to see urine in my life. He's weak still, but he's breathing much better and his skin is warm. I don't understand it myself. It must be some kind of miracle."

"I'll be damned," I say. "He's still putting us all through hoops, isn't he?"

"He knows you're coming, and he wants to see you," Sarah goes on. "I called Dr. Reilly to tell him that things were better, and he said he wanted to come out anyway, so I expect he'll be turning up soon, too."

I go through the living room and into Uncle Sol's room without taking my coat off. He is propped up on some pillows.

"Is that you, boy?" he whispers. "What took you so long?"

"You gave everyone a real scare," I say.

He squints at me and says, "What do you know—you're going gray, aren't you, Davey?"

"And no wonder," I say.

"Maybe you'll finally grow up after all," Uncle Sol whispers.

"I have grown up," I say.

"Yes, you have."

"Listen, let me take my coat off, and I'll be back in a minute."

"Is it snowing out?" Uncle Sol asks.

"Yes—hard," I say. "I was sliding from one side of the road to the other for the last five miles."

"Well, don't leave tracks all over the place," he says.

I stand there for a bit longer, and he seems to be drifting off. But then he says, "How is What's-His-Name—your son?"

"Charlie's just fine," I say.

"Do you think he would remember me?"

"Of course he does. Elizabeth and I were talking about having a party after Christmas and she asked Charlie who he wanted to come, and the first thing he said was 'Uncle Sol.'" Actually, Uncle Sol was Charlie's second choice; his first was the Muffin Man.

"Well, at least he has some intelligence, though I don't know where he got it from," Uncle Sol says, a smile playing across his lips.

I go back into the living room, where Sarah has settled down to her needlepoint. The long, bright-threaded motto has as its title "Friendship."

"That looks like hard work," I say.

"It's for my daughter's new house," she says. "She got married a few months ago, and now there's a baby on the way. Her pelvis is narrow, but the doctor says that shouldn't be too much of a problem."

I sit down across from her at the big table near the window.

"So what exactly happened with Sol?" I ask.

"Well, he woke up about twenty minutes after you called. He was just much better suddenly. I tried to get back to you, but your wife said you'd already left."

"Oh, that's O.K.," I say. "It's not every day that one gets to see a miracle, I guess."

"He said the strangest thing just after he woke up, though. He said he had been over there for a while, but that it wasn't time to stay yet."

"What?"

"He said he had gone over there for a while but the big boss said he wasn't ready yet."

The sky outside is low and portentous-looking, and the snow is being driven against the window by a strong wind. It makes little tapping noises, as if something were trying to get in. "The big boss?" I say.

"That's what he said. He said he'd seen his mother there, and then he began talking about the big boss again. I asked him who he meant, and he got irritated, the way he does, and said, 'You know perfectly well who I mean, young lady.' "

Out the window I catch sight of a procession of fat trolls on the lawn, way out by the gate that leads to the orchard. The shapes are blurry and dark and they seem to be an uncanny complement to Sarah's story, until I realize that it's just the wild turkeys again, trekking slowly through the snow as if they were on the last leg of some daring expedition.

"Oh, before I forget," Sarah says. "After you left the last time, your uncle set me to looking through his desk for a letter. He wanted you to see it, he said. I've kept it right there, on the table."

I pick up the yellowed envelope and see that it's from my
brother to Uncle Sol, and that the postmark says 1966. "Dear
Uncle Sol, I just wanted to thank you for talking to me for such
a long time about Johnson and our policy in Southeast Asia," it
begins. I don't really want to read a letter from a dead person
right now—it gives me even more willies than I already have,
what with turkey parades that look like they're out of the Twilight Zone and Uncle Sol's sojourn over there, wherever it was.

The sound of tires spinning on snow at the bottom of the
driveway provides me with an excuse to put the letter aside. Dr.
Reilly's car, the noise of its engine muffled, pulls up in front of the
house. The door opens and I see the doctor's long legs emerge,
but instead of getting out he just sits there, looking at the white
hills across the valley. He takes something out of his pocket, and
though I can't see it I know from the way his hands are working
that it's a rosary. When he has finished, he starts to trudge up to
the porch, and I get up to open the door for him.

"Hello, David," he says with a big smile as I take his coat.
"Now, don't criticize me—I said he could fool us. You'll have to
admit that sometimes there are things we don't understand. You
know, I'm so glad that Sol is not departing from us just yet. He
and I have had some long conversations over the past few weeks,
and I've been learning a lot from him. As wise as I am and at my
age—imagine."

"Yes, imagine," I say. "Excuse me for just one minute, Dr.
Reilly—I told him I'd go right back in to see him."

"Of course, of course—I'll just have a little talk with Sarah."

I am drunk with tiredness, and my back aches from driving,
and I feel grimy and aged, and all I want to do is call Elizabeth
and let her know what has happened, and ask her to call Ella and
tell her (I can hear Ella: "Oh, that's wonderful. What a relief.
Did Dave drive up there in this terrible weather? Is he all right?
The poor guy—he's going through a lot. Well, I hope the boy

is healthy. So long"), and then say that I'm on my way home and then actually *be* on my way home, and away from this hushed place and its surface neatness and its narrow thanatological business, and away from Uncle Sol and his chats with the big boss and his pausing long enough with one foot in the grave to teach a few last lessons, and back to the vital disorder of home, to my good wife, whose hostage I irretrievably am, and to my son, who is to me what hardware is to him. But no—not for a while yet.

Uncle Sol is half asleep and moaning a little. "I'm here," I say. "Are you in pain?"

"No," he mumbles.

"You were moaning, so I was wondering if you hurt somewhere."

"Yes," he says quietly.

"You *are* in pain?"

"Yes."

"Where?"

"I'm not sure," he whispers. "Somewhere around my backside."

"What's wrong?"

He opens his eyes, grins mischievously, and points a finger at me.

You have to hand it to him.

Vigils

SUN., Dec. 23, 12 midnite. I just took over from Janet. When she left she said, "Martha, I don't know if he can last the nite. Call me if you want company. I don't think I'll be getting much sleep." I think I will be okay. Sol is sleeping quietly. Resp. shallow and pulse very weak. Extremities cold to the touch, nailbeds blue. Oxygen on 3. I see in this log he hasn't been awake since I was here last and Dave came up to visit on Friday. Snowing out—it's beautiful.

CHARLIE HAS RESET THE clock again—a dextrous trick for a two-and-a-half-year-old, if I do say so myself. He presses his thumbs down on the small buttons on top of the digital clock next to Elizabeth's and my bed and watches time fly. Young children have no use for timepieces except as playthings, of course —they *are* clocks, in a way, and they live in an unenumerated paradise that I call Circadia, until they are forced to try to mesh their gears with civilization. It never works, though—at least it hasn't for me, because if it had, what am I doing awake at what the clock says is 12:15 P.M. when, I know, it is more like three in the morning? The lurid red numbers came swimming into my consciousness like electric eels from deep underwater, but now they've turned hard-edged, like the pang of sadness that has awakened me every few nights during the last couple of weeks, preceded by the same bad dream. On a Himalayan slope a small, misshapen biped of undeterminable species stares at me from a distance. It's like a *Traumwerk* Mister Potato, because it has had one different feature each time it has made an appearance—a nose like a carbuncular eggplant the first night, a rotten lily pinned to its chest a couple of nights later, and, tonight, guitars for legs. I can tell that it wants only to talk to me for a while—that there's no reason to fear it as it starts to hobble toward me over the barren icefield that separates us—but as it draws closer and as the loneliness that it emanates grows more intense, all I want to do is flee. At last, the creature stands shivering directly in front of me, and I can feel myself begin to absorb the coldness in its bones and the unhappiness in its heart, and that is when I finally take flight, by waking up.

It's not Uncle Sol. I mean, just because Uncle Sol always complained of being cold during his last few years, and just because he was a short, odd-looking man, and just because I did my best to avoid the "talks" he was always trying to have with me, and just because he played the guitar, grew lilies in his garden up in Sheffield, and had a big nose that couldn't seem to detect the near-putrefaction of warmed-over eggplant he occasionally served for dinner, and just because I think I might have done more to relieve the loneliness of his old age doesn't mean that that little hominid in my dream is Uncle Sol.

At 12:20 P.M. Charlie Standard Time, I sit up in bed, hopeless about getting back to sleep. Elizabeth, Charlie's mother and my wife—in that order, a little more often than I like—stirs. "The oranges haven't been delivered," she says. This is her unconscious trying to get her out of breakfast duty in the morning.

"Are the trees on strike?" I ask.

"Ha ha," Elizabeth says, turning over. "Maybe Marjorie will bring it." Marjorie is Elizabeth's mother. Elizabeth never calls her mother Marjorie.

" 'Them'—the oranges," I say. "Not 'it.' "

"Good," Elizabeth says. "File everything away."

"Right. Absolutely. I'll file it all away."

Elizabeth sighs a satisfied sigh and sinks back into a less loquacious stage of sleep, and I get up. I put on her bathrobe and cram my feet into her slippers. I consider ownership of these kinds of appurtenances a surrender to middle age, and, hovering around in my mid-forties, I'm still holding out. As I mince into the long hall, Charlie says, in a tone of happy awe, "Steam shovel." It's a chatty night for everyone but me. I go into the kitchen, pour myself a glass of Charlie's apple juice, and raid his animal crackers. Violet, our cat, black as the night itself, paints my shins with entreaties for food. When it becomes clear to her that I haven't donned Elizabeth's charity with her wardrobe, the cat goes away. I settle down on the couch in the living room and look out the window, which faces north and has an open three- or four-block view of apartment-house rooftops—cluttered, at this obscure hour, with dark, featureless forms, of water towers covered by yesterday's early-spring snow, television antennas encased in a thin coat of ice, steam pipes, and elevator housings—and beyond those small buildings taller ones, like suzerains towering over their supplicants. For a moment, I feel that I'm supposed to be keeping something out there under surveillance, and then the feeling turns into a conscious understanding of the preconscious memory that no doubt caused it—a memory of ineptly spying on some sort of food-processing plant in the Midwest when I was in my early twenties and shiftless one summer. I told Uncle Sol about the job last summer when he was depressed because he felt so sick and I had run out of the banter that I believed brought him some comfort. I knew it would bug him that I had done that—spied, and in the service of profit-hungry capitalists to boot—and it did. And it temporarily got some life back into him. It occurs to me now that he was angrier about what the tale represented—that I had my own life, a good part of which I hadn't shared with him—than about what it contained.

Thinking of food and capitalism, I bite off a lion and say to myself, enviously, Whoever invented animal crackers was a genius.

2 A.M. Sol still unconscious, condition same. Still snowing. I could swear I heard a door open and shut upstairs a few minutes ago. Hey, girls—anybody else seen any ghosts? David called about one. Said he couldn't sleep, just wanted to check on Sol's condition. He went over the instructions if Sol dies. He won't be able to come up, he said.

The Berkshire Community College spiral notebook that contains the log kept by Uncle Sol's nurse's aides lies like a mine under a pile of Charlie's word books on the end table next to the couch. I haven't been able to bring myself to read it even now, at the brink of full spring, three months after the old man's death. It was a peaceful departure, according to Sarah Deane, who was on duty and called me that Sunday night. Uncle Sol was in a coma and just stopped breathing, exactly as Dr. Reilly predicted would happen when I saw him at the farmhouse the Friday before, just as Uncle Sol was falling into his final sleep. If he had emerged from the coma, as he had once before, I would have gone back up, but he didn't, and I was tired, and Christmas was coming. I tell myself that I did all my leave-taking and grieving before then, anyway—weeping as I drove up to and down from the farmhouse four or five times in November and December; going teary over Charlie, so thrilled with life, on one of his naked scampers around the apartment after his bath; quoting Uncle Sol ("Clean as a girl from town"; "There is dignity in all labor"; "You should live so long!") even more often than I usually did.

I tell myself that—that I have by now felt all the sadness and that the relief of Uncle Sol's death dwarfed my self-recriminations—but I'm afraid to read the log.

Sarah showed me the notebook on that final visit to Uncle Sol. She entered into it what I wanted to be done when the end came, along with the phone number of the doctor who would be covering for Dr. Reilly over the weekend. She also took down the number of the funeral home in Lee with which I'd made arrangements for Uncle Sol's cremation on the phone and by mail and to which I had paid a call that day. The funeral director, Mr. Wczynczka, who had up till then been only a stereotypically unctuous voice on the telephone, kept on trying to interest me in "peripherals"—a viewing of the body for family and friends before cremation, flowers for the viewing, a mailing of death announcements. "It may not seem important to you," he said oleaginously, "but you should think of your father." He put his fleshy face, framed by the pilled collar of his polyester shirt and haircut that might have been done with a bowl and pinking shears, too close to mine and said, "For your father." I thought, I bet water would bead on your tongue, and also, Little do you know how contrary to my father's, to say nothing of my uncle's, wishes these ideas would be.

I told Mr. Wczynczka to hold the peripherals, except that I would like to see Uncle Sol before he was cremated. Mr. Wczynczka, who had until then been looking at me as though he had high hopes for me, looked at me now as though he had concluded that I would come to nothing after all but said, "All right." When I went up to see Uncle Sol, four days after his death, he had been laid out on a sofa at the opposite end of the stifling hot viewing room from a Mrs. Gray of Lenox, at rest in an elevated coffin for a service later in the day. In what looked like a fireplace a cylinder of thin metal with irregular-shaped holes in it rotated around an elongated light bulb the color of a pencil, casting fitful, aqueous orange illuminations on the walls—a Flamelite, no doubt, or an Emberglo or a Hearthmate. "I covered him with our afghan," Mr. Wczynczka told me. It looked like an old rug to me. Under a rug on a couch—I'm not kidding—but Uncle Sol would have appreciated the peculiarity of it all, and at least he was dressed in his one decent suit, as I had requested. "Now you'll want to be alone with him," Mr. Wczynczka said. He was back in under five minutes. Maybe Mrs. Gray's mourners would be arriving soon. But I'd had time to try to communicate my amusement to Uncle Sol, and my love, which had the purity that only death confers upon love, and to say, then, "So it's over," and kiss his bald head—impossibly cool, like marble, in that stuffy place—one last time.

6 A.M. *Sol's respiration so shallow that I have to check on him every five minutes to see if he's still breathing. Nothing else to report at this time. The snow stopped a while ago, and there's a little light behind the hills.*

A four-footed commotion in the kitchen—Violet acting up—brings me back from a reverie in which Uncle Sol reminded me that Mr. Wczynczka was simply a pitiable product of capitalism, ignorant in his greed for profit. Actually, the reverie turned into a dream, I now recall. I was back in college, feeling self-conscious because of my age. I walked into a classroom, and there was Uncle Sol, in black robes, about to begin a lecture. He took a look at me and said, "Shame on you, boy. You can't keep taking the same class over and over again just because you get good grades in it."

Violet, having catapulted around the kitchen for a few minutes, dashes into the living room and, using the cushion of a chair as a launching pad, springs up to the ledge at the top of the bottom windowpane. Her tail twitches a few times, and she exhales like an airbrake. The poor thing has felt beleaguered ever since Charlie showed up. For a long time after he started walking he chased her all over the place, and now he bawls her out whenever we bawl him out. She hides under the bed when he's around, emerging only after he's asleep. Charlie himself seems out of sorts recently, as if he knows that Elizabeth and I are thinking about another child. Or maybe he senses Uncle Sol's death. Kids do know those things, they say. He runs for his security blanket whenever we're stern with him—if he can't find Violet first.

Violet plummets down from her perch on the window and goes tearing along the hall toward the bedrooms. She often seems to lose something and run around looking for it at about this time of night, as I know from my vigils of the last few months. The first time I saw it, a week after Uncle Sol died, I was nodding off in the armchair, and I half-dreamed that someone had set a jaguar loose in the apartment. Some jaguar.

9 A.M. *The situation with Mr. Leonard is the same as it was with Martha. Very shallow resp., cold to the touch, feeble pulse, no sign of consciousness, not even when I attempted to arouse him by shouting, "Mr. Leonard it's Joan—Can you hear me?" a few times. Applied Vaseline to the lips and nostrils, turned him on one side a small amount.*

Elizabeth appears in the doorway, looking like a chilly seraph in the white nightgown that she's hugging against herself. "Violet just jumped on me," she said. "I swear. And you stole my bathrobe."

"What time is it?" I ask.

"The clock says four-thirty in the afternoon."

"Charlie."

"*Such* a cute trick," she says. "You can't sleep?"

"I slept until noon, but then I woke up."

"Thinking about Uncle Sol again?"

"I guess so, but not in any—you know, upset kind of way. Just thinking."

"Yes, well. If this winter ever ends, that will be a help. We can start working on the farmhouse."

"Oh, boy. Did I ever tell you about the wolves at Uncle Sol's?"

"There aren't any wolves in Sheffield," Elizabeth says.

"There was at least one, forty years ago."

And I tell her the story Uncle Sol told me in October, when he was in the hospital the last time. In the forties and fifties, his place in Sheffield served as a sort of summer retreat for New York City radicals who needed to get away from the routine of demonstrations and *Daily Worker* deadlines and FBI interrogations—a red-tinted, distorted-mirror image of the bourgeois rat race. When the house overflowed, Uncle Sol and the comrades would set up tents in the meadows behind the house. One time, a man somehow found his way up there whom despite his impeccable politics everyone found insufferable. He complained about the food, the weather, and the accommodations. He was sleeping in one of those tents. He was a great intellectual and had no patience with the romantic, unscientific Marxism of the other guests. "We wanted to get rid of him, but we didn't know how," Uncle Sol said. "Well, one day, someone remarked that our dog, Sammy, looked a lot like a wolf. You remember Sammy. You used to ride him like a horse and poured sand in his eyes from the driveway. A gentler creature you can't imagine. Well, anyway, when somebody said that Sammy looked like a wolf, I came up with a plan and I got everyone else in on it but this fellow Whosis. That night, I asked if anyone had heard the wolves in the woods behind the meadow the night before. Someone said he thought so but wasn't sure. We dropped it but came back to it every now and then. What's-His-Name was white as a sheet by the time we all went to bed, but he wouldn't let on he was scared. At about midnight, I and another fellow—Jim Something or Other—took Sammy up to the field with a big piece of red meat. We hadn't fed him that day at all, so he was hungry, let me tell you. When we got to this fellow's tent, I held the meat in front of the dog, and he growled. And he growled some more. Then the other fellow opened the flap of the tent and I threw the meat right through it—in one end and out the other. Sammy shot through the tent like a bullet. Jim and I went back down the hill to the house, jumped into bed and waited. Sure enough, ten or fifteen minutes later, here comes this fellow down from the meadow with his bags all packed. He got in his car and drove away."

Elizabeth laughs and sits down beside me. "I can just hear Sol telling that. What made you think of it?"

"Beats me."

"Why didn't Sol just ask the man to leave?"

"I asked him that myself. I'd never heard the story before, which is amazing."

"And?"

"Oh. He said that that wouldn't have been any fun."

6 P.M. Sarah here. Things are the same as with Joan and Martha. I think Sol has the beginning of gangrene on his left foot, but that doesn't matter now. He is doing Cheyne-Stokes breathing, and it can't be much longer now. David called and was confused, thought that Joan was still on duty. He reminded me to call Dr. Reilly first, in case he wants to come out instead of Dr. Seth. I sang some Carols to Sol, I don't care if it is foolish. I thought I felt some fibrillation in his pulse.

"Do you think I should have gone back up there?" I ask Elizabeth. "I mean, before he died."

"No. If you had, you would have found something else to feel bad about. It's a natural reaction."

10 P.M. Sol just passed away. Dr. Reilly will be coming out after all, to pronounce him. He went peacefully, with just some rales

*in his breathing before the end. It was just a sigh, really. Called
Mr. Wiżenski in Lee. Called David.*

*   11 P.M. Mr. Wiżenski just left with Sol. Will leave a few
lights on and lock the door. We came here twelve weeks ago
tonight. Hasn't been a fire in the fireplace all day today, so that's
O.K. As per David's instruction, turned the thermostat down to
50.*

"I guess you always feel that you haven't done enough, but
still, I wish I'd been with him when—"

Elizabeth takes the bathrobe off me, kisses me on the cheek,
gets up, and starts off toward the kitchen. Without turning
around—I can't tell if she's annoyed or amused—she says,
"Honestly! Don't you know anything?"

A NOTE ABOUT THE AUTHOR

Daniel Menaker was born in Manhattan, where he now lives with his wife and his two children. He is an editor at *The New Yorker*. Five of the eight stories in this collection originally appeared in *The New Yorker*; another, "The Old Left," was the winner of an O. Henry Award in 1984.

A NOTE ON THE TYPE

The text of this book was set in a digitized version of Fournier, a typeface originated by Pierre Simon Fournier, *fils* (1712–1768). Coming from a family of typefounders, Fournier was an extraordinarily prolific designer both of typefaces and of typographic ornaments. He was also the author of the celebrated *Manuel typographique* (1764–1766).

Composed by
Crane Typesetting Service, Inc.,
Barnstable, Massachusetts

Printed and bound by
Fairfield Graphics,
Fairfield, Pennsylvania

Typography and binding design by
Tasha Hall